ELIOT SCOTT

THE SINCLAIR HEIR

The Feud Series

The Sinclair Heir
The Feud Series Book 2
Text copyright © 2019

Ginger Scott, Anne Eliot
Writing as Eliot Scott
Butterfly Books, LLC
ISBN: 978-1-937815-17-2

Cover image copyright: Regina Wamba

Eliot Scott

We dedicate this to the old-school romance readers who miss the days of sneaking Mom's dog-eared paperbacks and reading them by flashlight.

PART II OF THE FEUD SERIES

NOTE FROM THE AUTHOR:

Before you dive in, we wanted to make sure you knew that this is part 2 in a two-book series. If you have not read The Wallace Girl yet, we strongly urge you to begin there. Things will make a whole lot more sense.

We hope you enjoy this thrilling conclusion to a story we have enjoyed from every letter and punctuation mark. Happy romance reading!

1.

JOJO, PRESENT DAY.

I can tell his lips yearn for mine despite what he's said.

He wants to kiss me.

He will kiss me.

I will *make* him.

I know in my heart that if he could just feel something deeper, the way our kisses always were and I know still are, he'd let go of those final pieces of ice he's holding up like a shield. I'm almost inside again, we're almost as we belong. But there is so much to untangle with him, so many terrible lies and threats we must undo. His father's rules—his *way*—poisoned him, and that evil runs so deep.

Alex's top lip has always had this twitch—a giveaway that says when he's about to give in to me. It moves now, and I stare and stare, willing him to lean forward. But instead, he pulls away, his body growing tense, like he might bolt. Dejected, I let my hands fall from his face and shift to his side, but that's when his fingers start to trail down my cheek.

Patience, Jojo. Be patient.

I freeze, afraid to push him too far. When my hair catches, he pulls in a sharp breath as he works to smooth it along my shoulder, and I wonder what he's thinking. So many hours of my youth were spent under the sun and stars with this boy, now a man, soothing my soul and running his fingertips through my hair just like this.

I glance sideways, peering through my lashes, and see that he's trying to regain the stoic expression he's worked so hard to maintain this entire night. I've seen him cry now, though, so that hard adult-Alex face of his, it's forever going to look softer to me now...it just *is*.

Loving how his hands feel playing with my hair, I remain still and let my eyes focus off of him and onto his bedroom. I'm searching for him, insights into who he's grown up to be, but this bedroom seems to be filled with everything that reminds me of *me*. My heart speeds up at the realization, and I know without asking that Alex—*my Alex*—made me this place, this room. Maybe it was a way to keep me in his memories, or maybe...just maybe...he hoped I would come back.

The bedding is white on white. Crisp cotton sheets tuck under a white ultra-thick cover quilted with white thread into small leaf patterns. Everything is overlaid with cable knit, a very expensive feeling cashmere throw that's now tangled around us both.

The entire room is a study in modern meets rustic. The bed frame is hand-pounded iron. The fireplace is ultra large and square, edged with a small band of chrome, and you can see through it all the way to what looks like a white marble tub next to a huge window. The floors warm it all up and balance all of the white. I can tell they're hand scraped. The wood is a gorgeous, wide-plank, reclaimed pine. It's the finest, I'm sure. I've only ever seen floors like this on HGTV. It's too dark to see outside the windows, which is frustrating because now I'm really curious where I'm at, so I let my gaze travel toward the door, hoping I can catch a glimpse of another room. Sadly, I can only see out into a dark hallway where the pine wood stops. I note the little black knots in the wood that match perfectly with the polished marble floor that picks up where the wood ends in the hallway.

"This room is beautiful. Did you have a designer help you decorate it?"

His movement pauses.

"No. I didn't."

I didn't think so. The details in here are too intimate, too perfect. This space is plucked right from my soul, the things Alex knows are so very much me.

I breathe in and let my eyes return to him and search

through my vivid memories from another time, looking for ones that will move him, convince him to kiss me. If I can get him to do that, I'll have him, and I will not let him go again.

"You remember when you proposed with that wire ring you made out of twisty ties on my parents' porch swing?"

I glance up and catch just enough of Alex's features to see he's staring at me again.

He doesn't respond, but he doesn't move. He feels this.

He feels this. My Alex.

"I kept that ring. It's in my jewelry box..." I hold my stare on his eyes, and he blinks just once.

"Did anyone ever offer you a real one?" He swallows and tries to mask it, but I see the movement in his throat.

I shake my head, no.

"It should have been a real ring." The tremble in his voice surprises me, the low timber gives me the urge to turn and face him all the way again. But I know that would be a mistake. I think he's on the edge right now. I also think I just heard his heart finally start beating through his voice.

"It was real enough for me," I press on.

"Like I always say, you deserve more. So much more."

I breathe out a laugh, because he's always said that to me, and because there was no *more* that Alex could have given. He gave me everything back then, and he's got no clue as to the *more* I've been raising for years without him.

The silence settles in again, too quickly. I feel him slipping away, and my mind battles with my heart for the right move to make, the right words to say. That feeling of desperation lingers. It always lingers.

"Why did you come back?" he asks again. "And don't answer that it's because my father died."

He settles in closer, his arms tightening on me, and I feel him relax just a little. My spine tingles with the breath on my neck when he speaks.

My pulse races, and my eyes close as I work to steady myself against the spinning room, him. Everything. I'm overwhelmed suddenly by how far I've come. It's starting to catch up with me, and I'm so tired of doing it alone I decide to tell him some of the truth. I tell him fast before I lose my nerve.

"It is because your father died. But that's not my reason. Yes, I knew it would be safe to come for you. But it's you, Alex. You're my reason. I mean it. I want you, and I to be together. I want us to have our future. I haven't been with anyone since I went away. You're my family, my home, and we've wasted so much time. You and I, we have something so very special—"

I feel the bed shift in an instant and he's so far across the room I could swear he flew there. "Shit, Jo! That's not the answer I expected."

"What did you think I'd say?" I'm hurt. My body's covered in goosebumps from the heat he took away from me just now, and from the fear that I almost just told him about Emily. It's too soon for that. He can barely handle the idea of me still wanting him.

"Answer me. What did you think I'd say?" I grill him again.

He starts pacing and his hands rub over his hair, then his face, his elbows going wide. It's the same pose he always struck when he would become frustrated. I've watched him pace like this over his father, over his mother...over Grady. Over me.

"I thought you'd say you were here to collect your aunt. To settle her into a retirement home, or to move her back home with you. I'm sure she's informed you how we practically held her hostage." He's reaching for reasons. I can hear how flustered he is, and I know he knows exactly why I'm here. He knew I'd come; he had to.

I nod. "She said a little about that, yes."

My aunt was *collateral*, but she wasn't as unwilling as the Sinclairs would like to think. As much as they used her to dangle a threat over me, she also spied on them and watched their every move.

"I want you to say you're here to sue my family for your lands to be returned to you. Now that my father's gone, his hold on the local legal officials will fade, and you can challenge all of it—everything was your mother's, and it should be returned to you. Hell, for that matter, I'll just give it all back to you."

"I don't want it. Not like that. Not unless it's both of ours." I level him with a steady and serious gaze.

"I just can't Jojo. I can't…" His voice is weak. His will is weak. He's giving in.

"But you do, and you can. *We can.* Or you wouldn't have just held me how you did, looked at me the way you did, or followed me and saved me for the millionth time from Grady. What I said was true—you're mine. You're looking at me and your expression tells me you're exactly where I am in your head, yet you're still lying. He's dead now, Alex. We can be together again. You're free…*we're* free."

"I'm not who I was. I'm not the guy you think I am."

"You are. You're that and more." I defy him, because I refuse to let him fall completely into the dark again now that he sees the light—I know he sees it.

His hands move from his face up into the thick waves of his hair, gripping as his eyes look haunted.

"I came prepared to fight for this. For you. I won't give up. I'm not the girl you think *I* am. I'm so much stronger." I shake my head and breathe in, forcing myself to forget the pain my body feels. The fuzz of medicine is wearing thin, and the blur of alcohol is faint.

Alex sighs, his shoulders slump but his frustration with me grows. His moves haven't changed, and I only need to predict them to break through.

"I can't keep you safe. Not now. Not after what just happened."

"So don't. I don't need to be safe. He's dead. *Dead*." I will have an answer for everything.

Alex laughs and spins slowly on his heels. When his eyes meet mine again, lightning strikes both of our souls. I feel it in my gut, and I see it shake him. His breath comes out fast, and his face falls to the right, revealing the exhaustion behind his eyes. They're red from his tears.

"You still don't get it, do you?" he says.

Our gaze locked, I sit up tall in the bed, wavering some as I get to my feet. I'm afraid that if I don't physically go after him, touch him, get him to touch me back again, that I'll lose him.

"Get what, Alex?" I step closer and closer, wincing as my weight challenges my sore and bruised legs.

His hands bunch at his sides as though he can't stand watching me wobbling around, as though he's worried I'm going to stumble and get hurt, but his eyes never leave mine as he says, "You don't get how much danger you're in. You don't get what this is…what you and I are wrapped up in. None of this was ever our choice, but it's too late, Jojo. We are who we are."

"We're two people who should still be in love. Who deserve to be together. Two people who got the shitty short end of the stick—who got played by our own families, and who went through a really dark time." I inch closer. "But that time, it's over. I'm here now. And you're here. And look at us—we're being honest...for once in our goddamned lives!"

Alex hasn't run away. Not yet. His brow crinkles and his gaze lowers away from my face when I stop only inches away from him. "We're Wallaces...Sinclairs...oil and water. *Enemies.* You can't love me, Jojo. It's impossible. After what I've done, you can't."

"We aren't enemies, Alex. We never were, and I don't care what you've done." My hand reaches slowly toward his heart. I press my fingers against him until my palm is flat on his white t-shirt, and my breath hitches with hope when he doesn't pull away.

"That ring you gave me had a promise attached to it. The lure you gave me says *forever.*" I peer up at him, his height always so much more than mine, and my tongue dashes out to lick my bottom lip. "I'm here for that."

His eyes are locked on my lips. I pull my bottom lip between my teeth, my mouth curving a hint of a smile as I shake my head, adding, "You once swore you loved me more than the sun. I know you still do. And I know it has to mean a lot to you that I never, ever stopped loving you."

I place both hands against his chest, and I feel his thundering heart. Alex's moan rumbles deep and near his heart before it escapes his lips along with my name.

"Jojo."

Alex's hands wrap around my wrists in an instant as though he means to tear my hands away from his heart, but instead, he just holds them, locking me to him. His eyes grow dark, and I can see the demons battling with the angels behind them.

"How you kissed me that night. How I kissed you back. Do you remember? Please, Alex. We're both so tired, and my body hurts as much as yours does. Just kiss me, take me back to your bed, and let's wash it all away. Please. "

2.

JOJO, JUNIOR YEAR.

"I'm sorry, Alex, but Jojo says she doesn't want to see you today," my dad says, just like we practiced.

I hold my breath behind the door, trying not to make a sound and give it away. My dad is somehow not breaking character either.

I lean over more to peer through the crack between the hinges, but all I can see is Alex's back. His hands are pushed deep in the back pockets of his jeans, and his plaid shirt is tucked in, just like it was at school.

I was supposed to get a ride home with Alex today, but when I got to the parking lot, Grady had caught up with me. He put his heavy arm around me and asked if it was over.

I didn't understand until he positioned me to take in the view of Alex carrying Molly Foster—*head cheerleader Molly Foster*, who is also one of the girls who tore up my dress sophomore year at the homecoming dance! She was his arms while he ran around his Mustang, and she was giggling and begging him to put her down.

Alex is playful with other girls sometimes. And other girls flirt with him a lot. Normally, it doesn't bother me because he always stops at a line, dropping everything and devoting his full attention to me the moment he sees me. Today, though...something was different.

I watched for a while, in the shadows, while Grady stood next to me. For once, Grady didn't seem awful, he only seemed sympathetic. He genuinely felt bad that I was watching Alex be so happy with this other girl. I got this thought in my head—*what would happen if Alex didn't know I was watching?*

I waited for several minutes more, and while nothing irreversible happened, the flirting did cross a line that I thought it never would.

I watched Alex set leggy, curvy Molly with her perfectly huge boobs and ultra-straight golden hair down on the hood of his car. Then he stood between her open knees while her skirt slid up just enough that I'm sure every guy nearby popped an erection. I felt my eyes begin to sting, as well as my heart. And when Molly reached forward and looped her fingers in the top of Alex's jeans, tugging him close, I gasped.

I guess I made a noise just loud enough to give away my position, because Alex's head turned in a jolt.

Our eyes met.

Grady grinned, then he shoved his meaty arm around my shoulder and whispered how sorry he was again. He said Alex was a dick, and that he'd kick his brother's ass for me.

I didn't want that, really, but for a flash of a moment I almost said yes.

It sucked. I ran home so fast that I didn't have time to cry, and somehow I skipped right over being hurt to being pissed off.

I knew Alex would come, so I talked my dad into tricking him, faking that it was some joke, only what my dad doesn't know is it's not really a trick—I honestly don't want to see Alex right now.

Ever again.

But then...

"Right," Alex says, his voice low and gravelly. He moves back just enough that I can see his profile. I lodge my thumbnail between my teeth and watch his body sway, his eyes looking downward, blinking with his thought.

"I messed up, sir," he says.

I move my knuckle in my mouth and bite down hard, leaning in the other direction to catch my father's expression. His brow is pinched. This isn't the story I told him of just wanting to prank my friend, and my dad is starting to get a sense of that. It's possible he knew all along.

"How so, son?" my father asks.

I lean my full weight into the wall behind me. It takes Alex several seconds to find his voice, and he has a few false starts before he begins to explain.

"Uhm…well…there was a girl, and I was just being funny, but then Jojo…or no…wait…not…"

"The truth, Alex. Trust me—the truth is always the only thing that matters," my dad tells him.

Alex breathes in deeply, then rights his gaze on my dad.

"Sometimes I feel like there are two versions of me. I know it sounds crazy, but…there's the guy I was supposed to be before I met Jojo, and then there's the guy I am, the one who…" Alex pauses, inhaling deep and holding his lungs full for a beat before letting the air fall away. "The one who loves your daughter more than the sun."

I glance to the right just in time to see a flinch of pain cast over my father's face. He hides it quickly, but it doesn't mean it wasn't there.

"And you messed up how?" my dad asks finally, urging Alex to continue.

"That other version of me…sometimes he forgets. It's easy to follow the blueprint. It's harder to color outside the lines, at least it is when Robert Sinclair is your dad. But that's no excuse. I got carried away today; there's this girl who I've known for years, longer than I've known Jojo. She's sort of…well…*open* with guys, if you know what I mean? And my brother was being Grady, and he told her that I had a crush on her, which I don't. But then I felt bad he said that, so I was…nice. Maybe *too nice?*"

"I understand. And for the record, I'm not really

liking how this conversation is going, Alex. I'm not so sure I want you to see Jojo either," my dad says.

"No, no. That's not what I mean," Alex says, his hands both coming up to rub his face. His eyes squint closed. I move back from view before they open. "She was waiting for me after school with a bunch of her friends. She's always been flirty, but usually I ignore it, but she had these stupid squirt guns, and when I told her to get off of the hood of my car, she started squirting me with them, and I picked her up and tried to squirt her back, and then she started giggling, and Jojo saw and..."

"I'm not sure what you want me to do for you, Alex," my dad says, and I can tell by the way my father's jaw is working that he's losing respect for Alex by the word.

"I guess nothing. I'm just so mad at myself because temptation got the best of me, and now maybe I've lost the best damn thing ever to live and breathe. I'm sorry, sir. Just...if you see her...tell her I'm sorry."

I watch my father for a sign, and when his eyes flit to mine, I know Alex has turned to walk away. There's so much in my dad's expression right now—warnings for his daughter, an itch to punch the boy who made me sad, but empathy for the version of Alex who tried to make it right.

"This is your call. One word and I'll slam this door shut for good," my dad says.

My eyes settle into his, searching for answers. When I realize there aren't any, I turn to my own heart. I swallow hard then nod.

"Hey, Alex!" my dad shouts. I step into the view next to him, and when Alex turns to face us both from his spot in the dirt walkway, he looks ghost white with both hope and fear. "Tell her yourself."

WHEN I REACH HIS SIDE, I pick up his hand. It's trembling, as is mine. "Want to go to the lake?"

He nods, his eyes taking me in, pouring over my face, his expressions as changeable as a spring storm. He's apologizing and worried, so full of love and so weighted with remorse that I can nearly taste every feeling in the world touching my face.

We don't speak during the entire walk to the lake.

We get to our rock, and I'm not sure if my lips find his first, or if his find mine. He mutters "I'm so sorry and I love you, Jojo" so many times into my mouth I'm full up with it—with him. I can't be anything but relieved, despite how I'm also still a bit mad at him, though I'm trying not to be. It all has me wanting to be as close to him as possible, so much so that I kiss him harder and push my tongue into his mouth as my hands trail up his shirt.

I want to forget our fight, but I also want him to forget the guilt that is part of him now that he made me so sad. And to be honest, I want him to forget the other girl. Nobody exists but me.

Trying not to be shy, I'm the first one out of my

jeans. I've unbuttoned his in seconds and I'm touching the hard, yet oh-so-very-soft-skinned erection I knew would be there. It always is when we're kissing on this rock. In his car. Stealing moments in the grain storage on the farm. Everywhere.

I pull off his shirt, and when that's done, I press him back against the rock. I sit with one leg on each side of him and balance myself over his hardness, pressing myself into him, gently yet more aggressively than I've ever done. I'm also pulling off my shirt, trying to get fully naked before he realizes what I'm trying to do and tries to slow us down.

"Take me, Alex." I say. "Make love to me right here, and right now. Please. Help me erase our fight—*everything*. I want to forget all of it right now and today. Your brother, my mom being sick—your messed up family and how our ancestors tried to hurt each other so badly. I want to take away how I can't understand why you're so dark sometimes, and why you always try to pull away from me."

I lean forward enough for my hair to fall against both cheeks, shading us and giving us a feeling of intimacy out here in the bright open sky.

"I want to remember only that we love each other. And I want you. I want you inside of me. I want every inch of your skin against mine, and I want you to try to feel my heart." I smile, biting my lip and a little turned on. The power of being like this with him makes me bolder, and I rub myself against him. I'm wet, and the heat makes me pulse deep inside. "Please."

He groans as his whole lower body bucks and presses up into me when I press myself down into him again before I unsnap my bra and toss it on top of where our clothes now lay, forgotten and crumpled together. We lick and we pant, and we kiss for a very long time as the most needy parts of our bodies work against each other, kneading with friction. His hands move to cup my breasts and pull on my nipples until they're tiny and pebble-hard, and I arch wishing I could feel just like this forever.

"You're so hot, Jojo. Fuck. I'm about to come just looking at you." His voice is so deep and growly, it makes me shiver with even more want.

"Don't you dare. Not yet."

"I can't do this...I can't have sex with you." His hands are on my waist, and suddenly he's pushing up more and more against me. His eyes are heated and nearly black, devouring me, so I touch myself while he watches.

"Why?" I throw my head back again, liking the feel of my long hair against my bare back. Knowing this move will jut my breasts up high, I wait until I feel his hot breath near them.

"First," he groans as I move my hands down between us so I can touch him again. "Oh—God. First." He places his hands over mine, forcing me to quit pumping my hand over his tip. "I don't have a condom on me. And..."

His eyes close as I push his hands off of mine to touch him again.

"And what?" I ask, loving how his face looks when I'm touching him like this. He's so open, and his sexy, curving mouth goes half open, reminding me of his kisses.

"And...this is not the time." His hands splay wide next to his body.

I move myself lower on him, and the hesitation begins to leave his eyes as my lips close in on where I know he wants them. He laughs lightly, a sexy one, his sweltering eyes meeting mine for a brief moment while he moves his head to the side, watching my lips going around him. He bites his smile and puts his hands on my head and deep into my hair, pushing down gently on my head as I take him into my mouth. Before I forget myself, and my goals, I pull off him to catch my breath.

"What were you saying? About why we can't have sex now?"

His face looks pained that I've stopped, but he answers with this sexy, tortured and gravelly voice. "There should be pillows for your beautiful head, and a mattress so your back won't get all scratched up and bruised. And music, and candles and flowers for your first time. Maybe a bathroom for you to use after, maybe a shower for us to get into *before*." He raises up one wicked brow. "I'm thinking it has to be in a fancy hotel that I pay for, and of course way more build up and way *slower* than how we got to this moment where we're both half dressed and desperate to make mistakes."

I frown at him, wondering if he thinks I was too forward. The word *mistake* hits my heart like a dart.

As if he can read my mind, he reaches up to cup his palm against my face and adds, "Hey. Don't make that face. I'm loving this moment—and I think you are too. It's the most epic make up, and I don't deserve one bit of it, but I'm also not going to just take your virginity when I still fill like shit for treating you so badly. Do you understand? It's not that I don't want you, because I want you so fucking bad every time you kiss me, Jojo Wallace. I just…can't. It needs to be special. Not here. Not now."

I pout, running my hands over his chest, and then trace each line in his tanned stomach before settling my hands where he's still so hard. "Fine. Then what can we do? Here." I squeeze him gently then threaten to let go. "And now? For me?"

"Let me show you." He pulls my body over his erection again and starts pushing upwards against my simple, cotton panties that are still on, and I start grinding down on him. His strong hands and forearms take over my entire weight. He's so strong he lifts me all the way off of him, and with seductive precision he starts rubbing me up and down against him in just my right spot until he has me moaning as much as he is. We both come fast, and we're both surprised by it, violently shuddering and shivering as we melt into each other at the same time.

For now, yes…this will do.

"Do we need to talk about it? Molly?" he asks, buttoning the last few buttons on his shirt while I tug my shirt down to cover my midriff.

I nod, wanting to just pretend it never happened but knowing that I won't do that, I'll hold onto it and use it to make myself feel awful. "Yeah. I guess."

"God, Jojo. I'm so sorry. You know I'd never do anything like that, or that Molly, she's just…one of those girls."

That's probably unfair to Molly, but I hate her right now, so I allow it.

"She touched you—you let her. It hurt. Bad." I keep it simple.

"I know," he says, suddenly not able to meet my eyes. I can't meet his. A part of me feels a little ashamed that I leapt right to making up before we had this talk. It was desperate, maybe.

"I didn't like it. I don't like her. I don't like you *flirting* with her or anyone," I say, my eyes on the silvery lake beauty stretched out in front of us.

Alex cups my face in his palms, tugging my head forward just enough to press his lips to the top of my head. "Never again," he whispers.

"I don't want you to even look at Molly Foster again," I say, half kidding, but only half.

"Molly who?" he teases, and I lean back to catch his expression. He isn't laughing as I thought he would; his eyes are serious...and still so very sorry. I stare into them for a long while as I feel the touch of his fingertips on my face.

"You told my dad you loved me," I say finally. Alex's eyes widen a bit.

"I did," he says, his lips pushing together tight.

"More than the sun," I say.

Alex nods. "I do. And you love me."

"That's, like...a whole lot of love," I say, tracing my finger along the flush in his cheeks, embarrassing him until his eyes fall closed.

"Right?" He says, smiling more.

Eventually, he cracks one eye open to look at me, and his chest begins to shake with his laughter. "Do you know how funny and special you are?" He pulls me into his embrace, the warmth of the falling sun painting us gold. "More beautiful than this sunset—than this lake."

"Do you want to come back with me and have dinner?" I ask, hoping he will.

"I'd like to, but I think after what I just admitted to your dad—and after what we just did here, on this rock —I won't be able to look that man in the eyes for days." Alex's lips set in a soft curve, the smile beckoning me to lean forward and press my mouth against his again.

He walks me all the way home, but he stops me just

before we step outside the shelter of the woods at the edge of our property. "Wait."

He pulls a rusted twist of wires out of his pocket that he's fashioned into what looks like a ring.

"It's ugly...and stupid. I made it when I was really upset about making you sad." He shrugs, but I love it instantly.

"I'll get you a real one someday, but...I don't know... maybe you can keep it with the lure. Or whatever." He glances down at me, his cheeks red with embarrassment. He pinches the makeshift ring between two fingers and lifts it between us slowly. "It's a desperate ring. I'm desperate. I just...I want you to know that you're it for me, Jojo. Whatever happens." His face grows tortured, those eyes of his pulling away and growing dark again. "Fuck. Whatever happens, I need to tell you that there will never ever be another love like what I feel for you. Not for me. Not ever."

"Me neither, Alex. And...this is so sweet." I take the ring into my palm, moving it around with my opposite hand. "And it's kind of...hideous." I snort a laugh, which makes him laugh too. "But love it. Love you. So much."

I hand it back and hold out my hand, letting him put the scratchy ring on my left hand for me. Just where a wedding band belongs on a woman's hand—where it will be one day for me and for him, I hope. I know we're young, and so much can happen before we're ready, but I can hope.

I wear Alex's funny ring and hold it next to my heart

as he stays in the woods while I walk, floating and satisfied but also blushing some as I remember how crazy things got out on our rock by the lake. I smile all the way back to my house all the same.

Once inside, I follow the scent to the kitchen where my mom is just pulling out a pot roast. My dad folds a towel on the table for her to set the searing-hot pan on, and when they peel back the tin foil, a puff of steam rises.

My dad glances between me and Mom, waiting as we all watch the smoke disappear along the rafters, then settles his gaze back on me.

"I'm guessing you two worked it out," he says, returning my huge smile.

"Yes." I flourish my ring out in front of them both. "Look. He gave me a ring. Sort of." I laugh, catching Mom's eyes going over my face. When she gets that I'm serious about the ring, her eyes flick to it and then back to my face.

She sways then, and seems to get momentarily panicked. Her eyes widen and she looks as if she's in pain, or really afraid. Her features pass through fright so quickly and then I blink and it's all gone. I wonder if I've imagined it.

I worry that she's getting sicker but trying to hide it from me. The doctors told me her type of cancer, at the end, really hurts. Dad has told me she's had some bad episodes while I've been at school this month too. It would so be like my mom not to want me to know, so I don't comment on what I think I just saw.

"You're very forgiving," my dad says, also ignoring Mom's odd lapse. He does step past me to help her to the table, something he's never done before. He returns to move the food to the table next. Even normal weight dinner plates suddenly seem too heavy for her. I quickly step up and help him carry the rest.

"He's very sweet," I chatter over the unusual tension hanging between us, and I'm suddenly glad that Alex didn't come back here with me tonight. He's right. This is awkward. "And...he was truly sorry."

"I'm sure he was," Mom says. "Don't let that ring cut your finger; it looks rather dangerous. After that lure-necklace you wear with the hook endlessly threatening to cut into your heart, I may have to ask him to switch to giving you flowers."

"Honey." Father admonishes her. "They're cute gestures. He's only a boy. We're pretty dumb sometimes. He'll learn."

"I hope so." Mom forces a smile, her expression though, when her eyes meet mine, makes me think that she's now suffering some terrible pain. "I was joking, Jojo. I simply hope Alex is not planning a career as a jewelry maker—his aesthetic is rather rustic." She laughs a little, as do I, but it's forced for both of us.

"The jewelry choices must be my fault. I told him to never, ever get me stupid diamonds. He took that idea literally and ran with it, I guess."

I've been nervously twisting the wire ring to rest looser against my finger, but instead it's gotten tighter. It's also turned my ring-finger black and it's chafed me a good amount too. I hide that hand under my napkin so they won't see, and I study my mom, taking in her nervous eyes, how she's picking at her food, and how she looks all slumped as though she's somehow deflated tonight.

My mom's hair has become thin, just like last time she was in chemo. She's started to shave what little is left. Sadly, the chemo's been over now for months, but her hair is showing no signs of growing back. She's still beautiful.

My dad makes a game of bringing home an endless parade of handmade caps and scarfs, and she's worn a different one every day this week. Today, her head is covered in mango-pink—the same color the sunset was tonight for me and Alex. The gifts give her some life, somehow. That small gesture from my dad seems to mean everything to her.

Tonight, though, it's making her look worse. She's more pale than ever, and it takes all my might to keep a straight face as I tell her how great her mac-and-cheese tastes. I swallow down the lump of fear that's rising up inside of me.

Since her diagnosis sophomore year, my mom's spirit has suffered. She was given horrible statistics of under a year to live, but it's been way more than that; she's heading into year two. And unlike the hair that won't grow back, her spirit has seemed to rally so hard that I guess I hadn't noticed the obvious—that she is getting weaker. I have this horrible feeling for the very first time since the cancer came back that maybe one day I'll come home from school to find her suddenly gone. It's inevitable, and I need to figure out how I will be able to handle it. How Dad and I will be able to handle it, because he's going to need me.

"Dear Lord," my father begins, and we all bow our heads and join our hands. "Thank you for this feast we are about to eat. Thank you for Jojo's happy smile at this table. And thank you for Alex, who's vowed to protect her."

I slide my foot forward under the table to nudge his. My dad nudges back, going on, "Thank you for our hope and strength. You've blessed my sweet wife with much of it. My daughter too. I ask you to give her a reprieve from pain and worry, and I beg you to choose me when one of us must suffer. Save her, and our daughter. My dear girls. Keep them safe, first...always. In your name, amen."

"Amen," we all repeat, and before my hand slides out of my dad's, he holds it fast, staring long and hard at the way the wire ring has done damage to my finger. When I pull it away, my eyes meet his, and they're deep and carrying so much sadness. I swear to God they're just as afraid as my mom's were.

But I'd swear they're not afraid for Mom.

I think they're afraid for me.

3.

JOJO, PRESENT DAY.

Patience is something I've forgotten how to practice. When I was young, I could spend hours staring into the shallow part of the lake, watching the fish and waiting for the perfect moment to strike. It's how I got so good at catching them.

I was always more patient than Alex.

Until now.

Our standoff slipped into a quiet, frozen state eventually, and the scotch pulled us into a slumber. It didn't last for more than a few hours for me, and I woke up in total darkness the first time, buzzes of texts from my aunt, wondering where I was. I told her I was with Alex, and that I was safe—I knew she'd know what it meant. My location app only connects to her, so if she really needs me, she can find me.

At that moment, she probably knew more about where I was than I did, actually. I tested Alex's sleep, moving first from his tender hold on the bed until I was in a sitting position, then to standing on my own. Every muscle in my body ached, and I bypassed the mirror in the bathroom, not wanting to see how any of it looked. I'm sure there are bruises, but if I see just how hideous I am, I won't feel like I can tempt Alex.

The faint ticking from a clock lured me out into the hallway, and my feet curled at the cool touch of the tile when the wood gave way to the slick surface. I looked behind me to make sure Alex was still asleep before flipping on the hallway light to take a better look at my surroundings.

The details hit me all at once. The floor was like ice, or more like water. Alex had brought the lake indoors, cresting the floor right up to the glass windows that were still too dark to see behind. Deep inside, I knew what was behind them. I just had to see it—had to smell it. I tiptoed to the door and slid it open after unlatching a very strong bolt. I held my breath, waiting for an alarm, but thankfully there wasn't one or Alex just never set it last night. I cracked the door enough to slip outside, and my feet found the familiar texture of wood once again.

The moon was high in the sky. The sun was still a few hours from rising, but the light was just enough to see. The deck was just as I would have built it, stretching far across the land and water, reaching to the very spot where Alex and I lived our lives. The sight of our rock— that Alex made it such a key part of this house—hit me in the center of my chest, and I rested my weight against the frame of the sliding door to take it in for several minutes.

Everything about that view is me. I don't have to ask him. I knew instantly why that view existed. It's so he never forgets what we were, and what we had. That view is proof that I'm here for the right reasons at the right time. It means Alex is not lost.

After breathing in the scent one last time, I returned inside, locking the door behind me. I touched everything on my way through the living room, and noted how oddly familiar every textile felt. It's as if Alex scooped up my future dreams and built them right here to live within.

It was all so much, and I was already overwhelmed when my eyes found a window to the past in the kitchen. Framed as if it were a work of art, the boards of my parents' farm house were displayed prominently. The char marks were removed, and the damaged wood was restored to the way it was supposed to look. The sight of it was almost too much for my tired heart to soak in, but I forced myself to sit there in the kitchen, in a chair I dragged to face it, for at least an hour. I sat there until I remembered everything, and then I let myself put it to bed.

I waited for the sun to rise back in the bedroom, and when it did, I felt refreshed, maybe even a little stronger than I was before I came back Tacoma.

Alex has been awake for a while now. I've caught him

staring at the ceiling, trying to keep a distance between us. I let him be like this, with me, for a while before I break the silence.

"Do you remember our first kiss? How I had to almost beg you to go for it? I feel like that's happening all over again."

Alex rolls his eyes then rubs his face as he stands and takes a few paces away from the bed.

"It's not," he protests, finally leveling me with his eyes, heavy with our past. "Why don't you remember our last kiss? Why don't you bring up the boathouse memories? You should hate me."

"I forgave you that night, and the memories I've kept from the boathouse were the sweet ones. Though, yes... you did throw terrible lies at me." I've practiced this. Self-therapy has gotten me here.

"Like the fucking wire ring, Jojo. You deserved more. You still deserve more." He lets out a sad chuckle and threads his fingers together, stretched across his forehead.

Everything in me aches for everything in him. My fingers itch to touch more, my lips quiver wanting to taste him, my body reacts as it always did, but it's my heart—it's always been my heart—that holds me back and needs this. I need *my* Alex. I can't love part of him. I need him whole, and he's so close.

So very close.

"Then...make it up to me. Give me more."

I stand and move toward him, taking careful steps

closer until our lips are nearly touching. I don't lean in because this has to come from him.

Alex's breath is hot, and his eyes haze when I press my body against his, and his breathing becomes more ragged.

"Make love to me. In your bed. Kiss me, taste me, have me completely. After we've had breakfast, we will talk about the rest of our truths. After you know everything, you can ask me to go. And I mean look me in the eye and honestly say you don't want me or what I'm offering you. If you can do that, I'll go for good."

"Let me get this straight. You want me to make love to you and you think it will be so good that I won't be able to walk away afterwards? Because *why*? Have you gotten so good from other…men?"

"No." I feel my face heating fire hot. "There have been no other men besides you."

His eyes flicker, and I recognize his jealousy fleeing. He's pleased. But it's also more than that. I couldn't give up on him, and he feels that too.

Unashamed, I capture his eyes and say, "I'm not going to lie to you, no matter how hard it seems, and you can bet your ass this is hard to say out loud, but since that day in the boathouse, it's been only me, myself…and every memory of you."

"Why? Don't answer that. I can't bear it if you say you had PTSD or that I fucked you up so badly that you never wanted to be with another man." His face grows pale, and I can tell by the tilt of his eyes that he's serious about feeling guilty. I'm sure on many levels, that's true —even if I wanted to, I probably wouldn't be able to handle a relationship with someone else without intense therapy. But I never wanted to try a different life. I've only ever wanted this one. And there has always been Emily.

I shrug. "No. None of that," I evade, feeling guilty. I said I wouldn't lie, but I never said I wouldn't hold back information.

When he only gapes at me, I press on. "I think you're afraid of me. Afraid of what one kiss will do to you. This act you have going, it doesn't add up. If you wanted me gone, you wouldn't have shown up and saved me from your brother's hands, you wouldn't have cared what he did to me."

He winces at my words like I've struck him. I can only hope it's a strike hard enough to make him finally let loose. The fire has grown in his eyes, and the longer I wait for him to react, the more his jaw flexes and the faster he breathes.

"Go on, Alex. I'm being honest, the least you can do is be honest, too. Say what's in your heart. Say I'm nothing to you, say those same cruel words from years ago, or that you want me dead."

His stare is ice cold.

"Do you?" I shove into him, knocking him off balance enough that he looks down at his feet, then back to my eyes.

He's breaking—Alex is breaking.

"How about you say that I'm just some stupid whore Wallace girl, that I'm nothing to you. Or better yet, tell me you hate me."

"No!" His hands push up my jaw and into my hair, and before I can blink, his lips press against mine. When I gasp for breath, his tongue dives into my mouth, his lips caressing, devouring. I step back against his force until I'm flush against the closed bedroom door. Alex's mouth is hard, yet so soft against mine, his body's heat making me melt. I push him away just enough for our eyes to meet, and I challenge him.

My bruised body no longer hurts. The only ache I feel is the one deep inside that wants Alex to complete me—to complete us.

Alex leans into me again, towering over me and caging me between his arms, his head against mine and his eyes closing as his hands slide inward until his right one finds my face again, his thumb caressing my jaw.

"Jojo." He says my name in this way that melts the back of my knees into rubber. His mouth dips down to my neck, and he holds his lips against my skin, dragging his nose along the curve while he pushes my hair to the side. His fingers find the scratches on my cheek, and he kisses against them lightly.

"I also won't lie to you again," he says, bringing his eyes back to look into mine. His hands move my hair behind my ears, and he follows the line his fingers take down my arms, slipping the shirt he dressed me in last night from my shoulders then moving to trace the edges of the lace that goes all the way around my bra.

"Lying to you killed me, and even though I should continue, I can't do it anymore. I can't because..." he pauses, breathing in slowly, his eyes raking over my how my nipples have gone hard underneath the lace from anticipation. I bring his gaze back to mine as I hold my palm against his face, the stubble from what I'm beginning to believe was a long night is rough against my skin.

"Because why?" I whisper.

"Because I'm weak. You...you level me. Completely, Jojo. You always have. Because you're the one I'm supposed to save, and I'm so goddamned afraid I won't be able to. Because I think I need you more than you need me. And because I'm giving in. I'm keeping you here because I'm greedy and selfish, because I want to taste you and have you, right here, in this bed. Because I want all of those dreams I've imagined having with you since we were fourteen, and fuck...I'm not supposed to have them, Jojo. I'm not. I should tell you to leave. I should make you, but I won't."

"Because I love you and because you love me."

"Goddamn, I do. Yes." He leans his forehead against mine again.

I slide my hands up his chest, my eyes taking in the man beneath my touch. "More than the sun." I smile wide.

"More than the fucking sun." He lightly kisses the bruise on my temple.

In a breath, Alex lifts me, and my legs wrap around his body while he walks us back to the bed. My back hits the mattress hard, and Alex crawls over me, his mouth finding mine, kissing me while he works me up the length of the bed, his hands tugging away the straps of my bra easily. He doesn't bother to admire anymore, instead letting hunger take over, his mouth covering my breast, his teeth biting down on my hardened nipple until I cry out from the raw pleasure it brings me.

My sound triggers something inside him, and his chest rumbles with a groan while he lifts himself to his knees, stripping away his shirt and unbuckling his belt, tugging it free, and unzipping his pants but leaving them on—a tease. I want more. He watches me as if I'm his prey, pinning me in place, my breasts rising with every breath, cold and wanting his warmth again, until another part of me takes over craving him.

Alex's hands work the button on my jeans quickly, and he grips the waistband hard, tugging my pants down my legs as he stands, leaving me in nothing more than my white, cotton panties. They aren't very sexy, and suddenly I'm ashamed.

"I wasn't prepared for this...otherwise I would have worn something different, like lace or..." I say, now afraid I've brought too much attention to my under-wear. I try to cover them but he quickly moves my hands away, letting his fingertips go under my waistband.

"I thought we weren't lying to each other." He stares down at me with eyes on fire.

"I would like to formally amend that during sex, sometimes we can lie." I gulp.

"Never." He laughs again, brushing a quick kiss over my lips. "You've always been able to make simple clothes like t-shirts and these," he pauses to reverently brush the back of his hand against my panties, "become the sexiest fucking things I've ever seen."

His hands slide up the inside of my calves, moving steadily up until he parts my knees. Feeling shivers down my spine, I gasp and fold my arm over my eyes, wanting to wait for the surprise of his touch as his fingers slowly tickle their way up the insides of my thighs.

I feel the bed shift beneath me as his body slides between my knees, his hands still moving until they reach the wet center strip. I feel his hand grip my arm, moving it above my head, forcing me to look at him.

"Do not hide that face. Ever. I've wanted to watch your lips quiver because of me for too long. Don't take that away now," he says, his eyes trailing down my naked body, his mouth falling forward and kissing my breasts.

"Okay," I pant, my hands moving to his hair, grabbing hold of the thick strands, remembering the feel of them.

Alex trails his tongue down my stomach, kissing my

belly button softly, his thumb hooking in the top of my panties briefly before his hand goes deeper to cup me completely. I arch my back, wanting more pressure as his thumb presses into my center, sliding up and down the soaking wet cotton.

"Fucking damn, Jojo. You're so wet," he growls.

I tremble when his other hand moves up my rib cage, stopping over the hard peak of my right nipple, his thumb rubbing in a slow circle, drawing my body up toward him.

He's like a magician, and I am his apprentice.

"Alex...please." I arch, as his tongue takes a slow swipe at the raw, pink tip.

"Please what, Jojo?" His mouth slides into a grin as his teeth graze along the hardened peaks. I've missed that grin, the way it could coax me into almost anything. It's the reason I gave myself to him in the first place.

"I want to feel all of you, deep inside. I need it, Alex. So badly...I've waited so long..."

Alex's expression shifts from playful to dominating, and his fingers curl under the band of my simple-but-apparently-sexy cotton panties, stripping them from my legs in a smooth drag that forces whatever breath I was holding onto to fall away. It leaves my lips parted and desperate to be touched. His hands trail up again in the same, torturous glide, until I feel his fingers gently pass across my center once...twice...then fall deep inside me. The burn is sweet, a faint reminder of how long it's been since he's been there—the *only* man to have ever been there.

"You're mine." The words slip out quietly, as if he's trying to convince himself that this is real.

"I am." I breathe out the words and dip my head enough to look him in the eyes—to *level* him, as he would say. It has always been Alex, and I have always been his. Why else would I believe in him so much? "Only you. Always..."

My words fall away as he pushes his fingers deeper inside, my back arching as his mouth covers my breast. Alex's hand moves at a steady rhythm, my hips soon following until I'm on the verge of coming. My fingers cling to the wrinkled quilt underneath us, but before I fall over the edge, Alex's hand moves and his body shifts until I feel his tongue press against my clit.

"Oh my god," I gasp, balling my hands into fists now, my head falling back as my eyes close. I'm unable to stop the eruption of waves that take over me completely, and my body jerks in response.

Alex's hand falls to my stomach, and he presses me flat, holding me still, forcing me to take it all, to ride every shock and tremble with each pulse as I orgasm.

When my muscles ease, Alex stands, sliding his pants down his legs and stepping out of them. His cock strains forward, and it's more than I remember, too.

I sit up enough to reach forward and grab it, bringing it to my mouth to take his length in until I feel it hit the back of my throat. His hands find the back of my head, and he slowly pumps in and out, my tongue working up and down his shaft with each pass.

"Jojo, *fuck...fuck, wait!*" he shouts, his eyes falling closed with the sensation.

Alex pulls away from my mouth and pushes me flat against the bed, then drags me down the length until my legs fall to the floor and he's standing over me. The movement hurts, but I don't care. I need him too much to let sore muscles and bruises slow me down.

"I have to feel you, inside of you, Jojo. I need to come in you..." he says, his voice hoarse, his actions forceful.

"Yes," I say, arching enough for him to find my entrance easily.

With his hands holding my thighs, Alex pushes into me, lifting me enough that he slides in easily and then out, stretching me open, diving deeper with every pump.

His hips fall forward into me harder, and I gasp, the sensation more than I remember. Alex leans forward, lifting my head, holding his body still until he gets confirmation from me that I want this—all of it—more.

"I'm okay. I'm just not used to you. My body...it's remembering." I pant out the words, not wanting him to stop.

"I'm sorry. I'll slow down." His eyes on mine, he rocks into me again, slower at the start, but faster with each push until he's entering me so hard that my breasts shake with the movement and my body moves up the bed.

Alex crawls to his knees on the mattress, still moving me with each push, until I wrap my legs around him completely, and he lifts my body against his warm chest as we move together. His hands slide up my back, fingers threading into my hair at the base of my neck. He's protecting me, and as his eyes lock on mine again, I realize that he's still trying to protect me from him. He wants *us* as badly as I do—I feel it in his gaze, in the way our bodies fit together like broken pieces of fine china. The fragments aren't perfect, not anymore, but the pieces would never be whole again on their own. They wouldn't be anything. They'd be discarded and forgotten.

Useless.

"You won't hurt me. Not again." I slow our movement and run my hands to his jaw, our eyes locked. I recognize those shadows behind his. His demons, they're never far. They own him. His parents—they made him. But I am the one who saved him. It's time I finished the job.

"You won't, Alex." His eyes become glassy.

"You love me." My own voice breaks, and his lips tremble, the corners giving way to a faint curve, his face cast in adoration as he nods and lets his head fall against mine again slowly.

"With everything left of me. There isn't much, Jojo, but whatever is...it's yours."

My body reacts, rocking with his again, our rhythm

steady, maybe cautious, as my heart opens itself to trust again and his begins to forgive himself for the past.

The first tear slides down my cheek seconds later, and Alex's thumb stops the second, kissing the evidence of it away. His lips find my ear.

"I'm yours." He whispers the declaration again and again, until his mouth can no longer form words, and my ears can no longer hear over the waves of pleasure pulling us in.

We both give in to the edge our bodies have been climbing toward. We hold on to one another just like this, him protecting me, and me protecting him, for several minutes. Alex eventually lures my body to lie with his, flush and still safe in his arms, our bodies drenched with sweat and a mountain of secrets to overcome.

4.

ALEX, END OF JUNIOR YEAR.

Grady intercepts me as I'm going to my car after school. "Hey Bro."

I nod, but look past his gleaming black eyes and scan the school parking lot for signs of Jojo making her way here, all the while hating the smug look that's been on my brother's face ever since he and father made me into a *good Sinclair.*

"Have fun cornering Jojo at her locker with your cheerleader bullies to make her cry again today?" I grit out finally.

"Hell yes I did." His grin grows wider. "She text you about that, the little cry baby snitch? Girl needs to get thicker skin. We were just joking around."

"She texted me that you called her poor trash this time. That this time you let those girls push her into her locker and throw wadded up paper at her. How in the hell is that any sort of joking around?" I drop my voice and try not to shout.

"Grady—*please stop.*"

I beg like I've begged him every damn day. Humbly. Eyes down, voice contrite, while trying to break into his heart. "Why do you have to do something mean to her every single goddamned day?"

I bravely look at him then and try to connect—this time it has got to work. "*Why* do you have to be Father's puppet in all of this? Don't you have a mind of your own? You're literally torturing her. She can't even walk down the hall and feel safe in class. Her grades are slipping. She's just a girl, and we're brothers, and I've begged you every day. Can't you at least back off of her here at school? No one needs to know."

He shakes his head at me like he's ashamed of my begging. "I can't back off of her. I'm doing my job, ass hat. What would I tell Father at the dinner table? You know he expects daily interactions on my part with your trash girlfriend. If I make her cry, Father bumps up my allowance. You get to play hero. She loves you more. We all win." He grins. "And fuck yes, I'll make fun that she's poor. It's an easy topic for an easy target. She's always wearing those cheap clothes, even the shoes from the Savey-Mart. How can I resist teasing her about that shit. She's trash to me; always will be. I could always scare instead. You know, by pushing her into the bathroom and cornering her for a little while? I'd like that..."

Bile rises in my throat as he laughs loud and long. "No. Whatever. Never mind."

He shrugs, blinking at me, obviously completely unmoved. "Father was right," he mutters. "You need to get your ass kicked so you can learn how to man up, boy."

He's said that last word exactly how Father says it. *Boy*. Like I'm nothing. Like I'm stupid, a bug to be squished.

I feel my chest crumpling in defeat, because for months, ever since they brought me in on their plan, I've been trying to work on my brother to soften. I even tried to beg my mother for some kind of help with our father's plans. I searched in her eyes for some sort of sympathy at least, because sympathy might give me strength when I find that mine is steadily decreasing.

I've received nothing from either of them, though. I get more of my mom's dead eyes when I try to bring it up. I get my brother's consistent responses, like the one he just gave me. I think that underneath it all Grady loves all of this, because he knows it's destroying me completely as well. They all know that they're killing me, literally.

I hurt so bad each day when I look into Jojo's eyes and tell her that I love her, because I do—yet I'm the one who stands by and knows that tomorrow Grady will hurt her again, or that my father will plan some stupid thing to happen in town that will make her upset or cry, or scare her mother half to death.

And I'm the one who hasn't told Jojo what's going on, because I'm too afraid of my father to do that. I just put my arm around her, hug her, love her, and hate myself more and more. I am exactly like Dr. Jekyll and Mr. Hyde, one hour a human, the next a monster.

They must know they're sacrificing me to this feud. I may not survive this. Something like this changes a person forever; it makes them mad from guilt and mental torture.

I've never fit in with my family. I've been told I'm a constant disappointment. I'm the one always reading, always fishing—always too sentimental and soft. I've heard that since birth from all three of them.

My family. What a joke.

Maybe this whole thing, in addition to the feud, is some sort of way of getting back at me for being the anomaly Sinclair. The only Sinclair in generations born with a soul!

I haven't had the balls to ask Grady—or any of them— if that's true. I don't need another beating from my father. Grady wouldn't understand the word *soul* because that concept is lost on him. And it hurts enough that my own mother just shakes her head at my tears, and tells me that this feud and Father's plans are "none of her business."

I look around the now emptying parking lot and check my phone for any texts, and my stomach drops, because I always drive Jojo home. It's not like her to go so long without at least checking in.

Grady's still standing here taunting me with his ever-widening and wicked grins, and I get a surge of anxiety. "Do you know where she is?"

He blinks at me innocently then answers. "Your little whore was picked up by her mother. I was out here, making sure they didn't miss each other. The woman needed a ride home from her chemo."

"Yeah, I know. Jojo's father always drives her."

Grady chuckles. "It appears our Father has an appointment with Mr. Wallace this afternoon, so he couldn't drive his half dead bitch around today. Jojo is going to stand in for her daddy while we all go up to the farm."

I reach for my cell and start typing a text.

"Don't bother." Grady holds up Jojo's cellphone and flashes it to me. "She won't text back."

"Why do you have her phone?" My heart thumps too hard into my chest. "What the hell is going on?"

"I pulled this out of her bag on impulse when I was helping her into her mother's car. I don't want to watch you two texting love shit all afternoon." He rolls his eyes, but he's a bad liar. His smirk gives him away.

"That's not why, is it? Why do you have her fucking phone?" I can feel my nostrils flare.

I reach for Jojo's cell, but like the ass that he is, Grady moves his hand away so I can't grab it away from him. It's exactly like when we were kids and he stole my ice cream cone.

"You'll give that to me, or I'm going to take it in blood. Your choice!" I grow bolder with my anger.

"Ooh. So scared." He pulls a face. "Of course I always choose *blood*. You can do your best to try to get it from me later."

He pockets Jojo's phone, and I feel sick.

I unlock the doors to my new Ford F150, a gift from my father because I'd been such a very good Sinclair. I hate it. Grady got one too. He loves his.

"What kind of appointment would Father and Mr. Wallace have?" I ask him, my mind buzzing with worry and running wild with ideas. Maybe he's trying to hammer out an end to the feud, or negotiate a trade for whatever he wants in exchange for letting us date. The sickness I feel in the pit of my stomach signals that I'm probably wrong.

"Family business." Grady's brows go up and down, like he's trying to be funny. "Father says I'm supposed to go with you, escort you in your truck, up to the Wallace place."

"Why would you need to go there. Only *I* go there," I stammer. The worry has grown into panic. This isn't right; nothing about this is right.

"Not today. Father's been planning this for weeks. And he's already been up there for hours, waiting with Mr. Wallace."

"Waiting for what?" My stomach swirls with nausea.

Grady opens his passenger side door after I've hit the unlock button, and as we get in and close the doors, he looks over at me with a stone-cold stare, but a sinister bend on his lips. "We're going to ramp up the drama here and kill Mr. Wallace today. Your job is to be present when Jojo gets home with her sick little mommy. You, brother, get to make it all better, as best you can."

He shrugs, then laughs as if this is all pretend. I fire the engine as I look over at him, working hard to hide the shaking in my hands as I try to call his bluff, but I know this is real. Grady is not the creative type. He wouldn't be able to think up saying the words he just said to me on his own.

I force an eye roll anyway, and put the truck into reverse, adding, "Shut the fuck up, Grady. Stop kidding around. What are we really going to do?"

I look him in the eyes before I push the gear into drive. Grady's expression turns serious. "I said we're going to kill Mr. Wallace today. It's your damn fault. You've been bull-shitting us. We know you've been pretending you're all in and then talking to Mother behind Father's back. You've been ditching class to protect Jojo and thwart my plans to mess with her head. Father isn't happy about any of it. Oh, and I had to tell him all about the billions of times you begged me like a little pussy—just how you did today...again—to go behind Father's back and try to deviate from his plans. You're a selfish little baby-fuck, and now you're going to pay for it."

He shakes his head at me, his expression wavering towards pity but ending on his usual disdain. "Did you not think Father would find out. He can read our minds, you idiot. And your mind has been screaming since homecoming. Now drive the truck to the Wallace farm."

I drive, my eyes scanning for places to turn quickly and escape, but a part of me still thinks he's kidding. When I'm forced to stop at a red light, I prepare myself to challenge him one last time. My words never leave my lips this time, though. He's got a gun trained on me, aimed at the deep center of my body. And it's not just any gun. It's our father's 44 Magnum, a gun we're never allowed to touch. Ever. It was a gift from the police department; they gave it to Father after he supplemented their pension—*after he bought them.*

Grady's grin and his cold-sparkling eyes speak for him, and I know beyond doubt now that killing Mr. Wallace is actually today's plan. He stole Jojo's cell phone to make sure I don't interfere or text her. He's been laughing in my face this whole time I've been begging him not to mess with Jojo in the school.

I swallow hard, a thousand needles scratching my insides on their way down. My heart sinks and my mind reels.

This is my fault.

I should never have trusted our mother. I should have known she would tell Father I was resisting. I let them see me cry and beg, and that was a mistake too. They know I'm weak. I've learned nothing from being a Sinclair.

"I won't do it. I'll stop you guys from doing this," I

utter out, pissed off that my voice is shaking. I'm not as brave as I should be.

Grady waves the gun at me, then jams it so hard into my stomach that I nearly double over as the air goes out of my diaphragm. It's worse than taking a punch.

"Father said you'd say that. He told me to do this." He shoves the gun harder into my gut with all of his might, causing both me and him to grunt. "He says if you want Jojo and her mother to live out the day as well, you will do exactly what we say. And then we will leave the farm, and you'll stay there, waiting for Jojo to get home. You'll pick up all of the pieces, and you'll put her back together how you do. Unless you want to die today and let Father and I handle those sad little pieces of Jojo ourselves. We could always do it *my way.*"

The light changes, and I start driving again, towards the Wallace farm. If it were only my life, I'd veer off the road and kill us both. But my father is still there, and he can still do more damage.

Grady doesn't take the gun pressure off my gut, and I get my shaking under control. I shove down my tears and swallow down my nausea. I'm done being afraid of them. Done feeling sorry for myself.

I will find a way to stop this today.

I will.

To ignore the pain of the gun Grady's got shoved into

my diaphragm and the terror attacking my soul about this plan to kill Mr. Wallace, I've been commanding my mind to stay calm and focused by inwardly chanting: *I will save Mr. Wallace. I will. I will stop this. I will save Mr. Wallace... I will keep Jojo safe. Today. It all stops today.*

As I park, Grady pulls the gun out of my gut. There is little relief.

I'm finally able to draw in my first full breath, but it's ragged because this kind of fear fucking hurts. I've parked my truck right next to where Father's too-shiny black Lexus is hidden behind the back entrance to the larger granary on the Wallace farm.

I look up to the top of it, brushing away the empty wheat hulls that make up the swirling air around here. I'm trying to picture what Father and Mr. Wallace are doing up there right now. This granary was filled nearly to the top with wheat by the last farmers wanting to store for winter, and that was only a week ago. It's not comfortable in there when it's full. The air is too thin and the space feels muggy, and I think it's the last place my father would want to hang out for an entire afternoon.

It also makes me wonder if what Grady has told me might not be true? Have Father and Mr. Wallace truly been up there for *hours?* To me, this plan doesn't seem like Father—not at all.

Poker-facing it, I stare around the farm, waiting and hoping Grady is full of shit and that he will finally call the bluff. *God*, I pray silently. And then I pray harder when Grady's eyes start to flicker with some sort of dark and secretive happiness that I simply can't understand. *Please—please—let it all be some sort of bluff. Please, God...please.*

My gaze flicks wildly around the property in search for some sign, some spiritual answer. I'm now hoping to find Mrs. Wallace's car coming up the drive, hoping to hear the crunch of a neighbor's vehicle approaching to say hello or at least bring me a distraction so I can run and gain time to figure out what to do.

Fuck. I'm hoping for the mailman...anyone! But there is only more wind, more wheat hulls cutting into my eyes, and fucking stupid-ass Grady. He's kept his gun out and pointed at me and when I'm still motionless, he sighs like I've annoyed him and he jerks it in the direction of the long metal staircase leading to the top of the granary.

"Dude. Get up there. I told you Father's been waiting. You lead up the staircase. All the way up."

I roll my eyes at the gun—and at him—acting like he's an idiot. I act like I don't think he'll use the weapon on me, but my whole body knows deep down that today he will. A part of him has always wanted me dead, I think.

As I start up the steps, they clang and bang beneath my feet. I want Mr. Wallace to know I'm coming. I want them to hear me coming...in case it may somehow help.

Help. Help. Help.

The word ping-pongs around my head, mocking me.

To stay strong and focused for whatever I might see up inside the granary, I force away ideas of Mr. Wallace already hanging from a rope. I ignore my ideas of Mr. Wallace beaten and bloodied by my father, and force myself to picture even worse things.

Things about Jojo. Things that they will do to her if I mess up today. I make myself see my own Father wrestling with my girlfriend, hitting her how he hits me, fucking her how he threatens to do.

I picture myself held in Grady's vice-grip while Grady and I watch this happening. I see Jojo's mom—weak and broken from her chemo appointment—trying to stop Jojo from being hurt, and getting kicked to the dirt by my father's boots.

I make myself imagine Grady "having his turn" with Jojo's broken and sobbing body, just how he's wanted since this all started.

I make it worse and worse, imagining Jojo's screams and cries over and over inside my head as I near the top.

I feel sick.

If you fail, Alex Sinclair...if you slip up—if you say the wrong thing—if you do the wrong thing and get yourself killed today, then Jojo and her mom will hurt more than you can imagine. Don't forget that. Whatever Father and Grady are doing here, don't forget Jojo. Stay focused.

As we reach the top steps and walk onto the long metal landing that leads to a narrow door and the internal walkways inside, I glance back at Grady—at the gun. I imagine myself pulling the gun out of Grady's hand. I picture myself shooting Grady in the head, and then envision turning it on my father.

I'll do it fast. I'll do it before Father ever sees it coming. If these people, my family, are serious, then I'm serious too.

This—the feud—it will finally be over.

I will kill my father. I will kill my brother.

I will confess that I did it.

I will be just as happy about my plan as they are about theirs.

I will. I will stop this.

I will, I will, I will...

"What are you waiting for? Open the door, *Jackwad*! I hate being up this high," Grady commands.

"I can't open it at all if you're trying to put your dick up in my ass, so move the fuck back," I growl back at him, acting annoyed. I act just like Father. I've already decided not to make a grab for the gun. I can't afford to be impulsive just yet. I need to figure out if Mr. Wallace is still alive.

Grady half clocks my head with the gun as he reaches over me to use the gun to bang on the metal door, muttering "oops" as though that hit was an accident while shouting the obvious "Father. We're here!"

"Come on in. It's secure." My father's muffled reply comes through the door.

Grady finally steps back as I'd asked him. He watches me carefully as I press the handle down hard and pull the door open wide and fast. I step in quickly and am able to get my bearings fast—I've been here. But when I realize what's really happening, my heart sinks. My soul dies.

Father's on the mirrored platform walkway, the one that's directly across the way from where Grady's keeping me at gunpoint. My mouth must have dropped open in surprise, and Grady, who has been watching me, lets out another snide and cruel laugh.

"Fucking *dumbass Alex*...close your mouth before some flies head in there." He cackles again. "You're so easy to fool."

No...no. No wonder Father's voice had sounded so muffled. He's on the other side.

Father's leaning over the metal railing, and his elated smile matches Grady's, his laughter just as cruel and delighted, as though he knows I've just realized they've rattled me. They tricked me again by the simple act of parking the car by the door on the far side.

Not that I'd had the choice as to which staircase I could go up, all thanks to the gun. But Father had obviously wanted me to think he was holding Mr. Wallace hostage on *this* side. Father had wanted me to think that maybe I could change things. Stop it. When now, it's obvious that I can't.

The only way to get to where they are—the only way to try to stop this—is if I were to dash out of this door, run down the steps and then run up the other side. They know there's no time for that. Even if I managed to break free, it would be too late for Mr. Wallace.

Too late for me.

Way too fucking late.

Holding myself deadly still, I allow my eyes to meet Father's, then Grady's. Their smug satisfaction and obvious delight at how this is playing out is like a throat punch. I can see myself inside their eyes. I'm like a dog that just keeps coming back, hoping to get petted, even after it's been kicked and kicked.

Grady gently places his gunpoint on my temple. No bruising pressure needed. No more head smacks. Only cold, hard steel against the exact spot that is throbbing with my rapidly dying heartbeats. This is the exact spot where the blood in my veins has just turned to ice.

I get what's happening and why.

This is my fault. I've been so naive.

As though Father can read my mind, he asks, "Did Grady *explain* everything to you, Alex? *Why* we are at this point in our little game? *Why* we are taking this drastic step with our dear friend here? *Why* Mr. Wallace must die earlier than expected?"

I don't answer him yet, because I've finally noticed that in addition to his own gun—one that he's pointed at Mr. Wallace—Father's also been holding one of the oversized wrenches Mr. Wallace and I use to tighten the bolts of the walkways each year.

Last night at dinner, I mentioned those huge wrenches to Father. I told him that I'd be up here working today. *"I'm helping Mr. Wallace winterize the granary again this year,"* I'd said.

Father had been so curious as to what that meant, exactly. I fucking gave him the details. I told him we only had to tighten the bolts on the *right side* of the granary walkway, the ones that always seem to become loose after the heat of the summer. The foundation underneath has settled over the years, I'd explained.

Fuck! I'd gone on and on. I'd even told Father exactly how dangerous the walkways could become if the bolts stayed loose.

The whole end of the walkway could go down into the grain...

The right side...

Right side of the granary walkway...

Where they are standing now.

Where I can't get to in time even if I could fight Grady and run.

I gave Father this idea. I should have known. I should have been better, smarter—understood. They always say I'm so stupid, and they are right. I am.

Father chuckles with manic delight.

"I've told Mr. Wallace here that you're very sorry about it all. That you didn't *mean* to directly go against your father's wishes, but that you did, and that you have done so for too long now. He understands parenting and the need for proper consequences. I also told him that today is the day of reckoning. This is *your* punishment, Alex. Even more than this bastard's punishment for stealing away my fiancé. Because all of this, it's really all her fault, isn't it? That whore! Fucking Wallace girl that she became. She took my ring, she made me a promise and then she broke it, didn't she?"

His voice cracks with half-bitter sarcasm and half sheer-Sinclair fury.

"*Changed her mind,* she'd said. But see, I never changed mine. And I still want back what was supposed to be mine. What she's held hostage from me, and what she *refuses* to give back! She's thought all along that move had protected her, protected her family. Her husband and her little devil's spawn. That's always been her bargaining chip, but she's got no clue that I've been planning this murder since the day of her wedding. I gave her the chance to return it, but now she will give it all back to me—and on *my* terms now. One drop of her family's blood at a time. And you, Alex and Grady—my sons—you're going to help me right this wrong."

5.

JOJO, PRESENT DAY.

I almost forgot what it feels like to wake with nothing but a lakeside breeze tickling your face and tangled sheets keeping the chill from your bare legs. I haven't slept so still, so peaceful, since I was a child.

Since Alex and I were innocent best friends who liked to splash each other in the water and gross each other out with fat worms smooshed on the wooden planks of our favorite pier. One kiss, and I never truly felt safe to sleep alone again. I gave the safety up gladly, though, and I'd do it all again for him. The heart wants what it wants, and Alex makes me believe in things like destiny. He and I are the answer to nearly a century of deceit and lies, the place where our twisted family lines begin to weave together.

My eyes linger on his back. I knew the moment he woke up and slipped out of bed. It's colder without him.

"You've always loved staring at the water." He doesn't flinch at my words. He knows I've been watching him.

Alex's shoulders rise slightly with a breathy laugh.

"It drove my father nuts when I'd do this," he says. "He said I daydreamed, and maybe that's what it was. I kinda think I was escaping, though. I don't know…" His words trail off.

I slide from the bed, wrapping my body in the silky cream sheets. Alex turns, making room for me on his lap, so I sit to stare out at the water with him. The way the light plays off of the ripples, it looks like thousands of diamonds. Fitting, since the riches of the world are in that water. You control the water…you control the world.

"Remember the underwater world we were going to build?" I ask.

His chest shakes against me with his laughter. "'Just keep digging!' You would yell that every time I tried to talk you into giving up."

"No matter how deep we tunneled on the beach, the water would just flow right in." I roll my eyes understanding the physics better now that I'm an adult.

"I wanted to build that tunnel for you," Alex hums, his rough cheek scratching against my bare arm as he rests against me, sliding his hands around my body.

"You built me this instead." My eyes wander to the side, looking at the details that were so obviously meant for my attention, from the buttercup yellow window seat and wall of books to the soaring ceiling beams, knotted and stained by hand. I know without asking that Alex was responsible for that part. He was always so talented with his hands. In another life, he would have been a carpenter. Instead he was a prisoner.

"I put this window here under the delusion that one day, I'd watch the sun rise with you, right here…just like this."

I feel him take in a heavy breath, so I turn and wrap my arms around him, our eyes meeting.

"You say delusions…I say faith. You had faith, Alex." My chin drops as his rises, and our lips brush lightly.

"I have faith in you," he whispers the words against me.

My mouth curves in reaction. I arch my back and roll my shoulders, testing the tenderness of my muscles. The soreness is there, but not as bad as I thought it would be. Perhaps it's just blinded by bliss.

"Come, let me make you breakfast." He grips my waist and lifts me from his lap, but holds me close as he rises. His boxers hang low on his hips, and my thumbs automatically go to the band, dipping in and teasingly tugging them lower. His hands slide down my arms to my wrists so he can stop me.

"Jojo, if you keep that up, we'll never eat. And I really think you need something for breakfast, after every-thing." He brushes his nose against mine sweetly then smirks with one brow raised.

"Fine." I pout, but my tummy is rumbling. And I can feel the sting of a buried headache deep in my temples. Some food and coffee would probably cure some of that.

Alex backs away from me, and I stand, wrapping the sheet around me completely as I reach for the T-shirt left sitting on the dresser's top. Just before I grip it, Alex snags it and throws it over his shoulder.

"Hey." I giggle.

"I laid that shirt out for you before you teased me this morning. Now, I think it's better that you stay naked." His eyes dance with want, and I feel it between my legs. I knew when I finally had Alex again that my heart would be full of love. I didn't know how sexy he would make me feel. I didn't know how addicted I would become to his touch and to feeling him inside of me. I didn't know I'd be beholden to him so fast. I am, though—completely.

My lip rises on the right and I let go of my hold on the sheets enough that they slip down my body, uncovering my right breast, the nipple hard with desire.

"Goddamn," Alex says, his tongue passing slowly over his bottom lip just before his teeth bite down.

Alex's eyes drag from my naked chest up to my eyes, his dimples deepening as he walks backward and curls his finger, calling me to follow. I obey, letting the sheet go completely by the time we leave his bedroom. The air is cool, which only makes my nipples harden more, and I decide to keep them—*all* of me—in Alex's view as he rounds the kitchen island and forces his attention to a pantry cabinet near the stove.

"You always loved pancakes, and that's about the only thing I really know how to make." He laughs at himself, but keeps his focus on the stove in front of him, tearing open the cardboard lid of the pancake mix he has clearly never used. I'm guessing pans are under the island, so I lift myself up to sit with my legs crossed, blocking his way into the doors. It only takes him a few seconds to turn and notice.

"Ah...seductress," he says, breathing out a defeated laugh and giving in to temptation just a little as his palm finds my right knee and slides until it cups it completely.

"Am I...in your way?" My lips pucker with my smile, and my whole body throbs from the sweet torture.

"Not at all." Alex's eyes steady on mine and his chin lifts ever so slightly as the grip of his hand on my knee tightens. His hand moves to the inside of my thigh and he uncrosses my legs, and soon I feel the graze of his other hand on the inside of my opposite leg. His thumbs circle against my delicate skin for a few seconds, lulling me and making me wet, then Alex jerks my legs open wide and sneers at me, forcing me to gasp.

I pant twice, hard, my nipples reaching for him, my fingers curling against the counter, wanting to pull his cock out and guide it inside of me. Alex's hands inch up my thighs until his thumbs tickle against the soft pink of my center. My head falls back, and I whimper. His touch is feather light, and completely still. One roll of my hips would press his fingers into me, but I can tell he wants to be in control of this, so I wait.

His thumb glides up my clit once, stopping just a thread away from the most sensitive and hungry spot, and more seconds pass. I squeeze my eyes closed and curl my toes in anticipation, and am rewarded with a flick of Alex's tongue against the hard peak of my breast.

"Ahhh." That small touch sends shivers through my body all the way to my swollen pussy, and Alex's thumb circles my soft skin again, covering me with my own wetness as vibrations sear through my core.

"Alex, oh God!" My fingers splay on the counter and I slide back a few inches as my body shudders in response. His thumb presses into my clit, his force growing with each wave that passes through me until my knees lift from the uncontrollable convulsing. I come hard from this sexual torture, and I lie back flat on the counter, my smile wide with my own surprise.

"I just need in here," Alex says, his wet fingertips grazing down my thighs and knees until I hear the sound of the cabinet door open beneath me.

Fucking hell. I'm out of breath, and my face is flushed. I didn't know it was possible to orgasm so hard from just a simple touch. I want to spend days being satisfied like this. I want Alex to do it again, right now. I want him to fuck me then taste me, then cover me in himself. One night, and he's turned me into a woman on fire.

"One pancake, or two?"

I don't answer right away, stunned by the question, and I finally just laugh.

"Two!" I chuckle, pulling my knees up into my chest to squeeze away the lasting pressure deep inside. I rock myself up, and as I do, Alex looks over his shoulder and raises his lip again, this time in pride.

"We're not done." His eyes smolder, lowering to my still hard nipples, and just this look alone makes me nearly come again.

As PROMISED, I remain naked through breakfast, and I think the only reason I was able to eat any pancake at all was because Alex insisted we go outside, to the porch and long-stretching deck. Something about being here—staring at our rock, our water and our past—makes it easier to wait. We've waited so long already.

I set my plate down ten minutes ago, and Alex took it inside soon after. I found my way to our rock while he was away, and I've been sitting here ever since while he watches me from the other end of the deck.

"There's room for two over here, you know." My hair falls over my shoulder as I turn to him, the waves blanketing one breast.

There's also something about Alex's expression that's missing from earlier, though, and I can tell that no matter what I do to tempt him right now, he won't be here with me completely. My Alex is battling internally with the tortured one who doesn't feel worthy.

"All these years, we could always talk. It just wasn't always the truth, but I think we're past that now, don't you? It's time for honesty. It's time for *real*, Alex, because we deserve that, don't you think?"

I curl my legs in and square myself with him. A soft smile paints his face but fades as his eyes gloss with worry. Even from several feet away I can see the harsh swallow that strangles his throat.

"Tell me. Whatever it is. Whatever you think will happen, tell me. We can find a way to defeat it."

My resolve is met by his weakness, and a soft laugh curls his mouth as his eyes close.

"You have no idea how bad it is, Jojo. And you are so beautiful, and I want you so much—love you so much— that I just took you. I took what I didn't earn, because I'm a monster. Like all the Sinclairs. If you knew it all, Jo...if you knew..."

My stomach twitches nervously and my skin rushes with a numbness. I push it down, though, ignoring the instinct to run from this conversation. If we're to be anything at all, we have to know everything. There is no room for secrets.

"So tell me, because I think I already do know," I say, shifting enough to the side to make room for Alex next to me. He looks up and shakes his head, so I insist. "Don't you dare be afraid now. We've been through too much. Come...tell me what you're thinking."

His chest lifts with a heavy breath, and slowly, he walks closer. I reach for his hand when he's near enough, and I hold it in mine while he sits on the rock with me, his body turned so he isn't forced to look in my eyes. He's avoiding, and I know I'll need to force him to confront this hurdle. I move closer to him and cup the side of his face, nudging him to look at me until our eyes lock, and the absolute terror reflected in them practically drowns me.

This is about my parents—about the day my father died. This is his misplaced guilt, and it's what I always knew but never told him.

"Stop punishing yourself," I say in a soft voice.

His face tenses and his jaw flexes in resistance. "Jojo, you don't know what I've done—seen—participated in to hurt you."

"Alex..."

I turn into him more and grasp at the plain, white T-shirt he put on before we came out here. I hold the cotton in my fists and plead with his eyes. Alex smells like amber and the woods around us, and I'm dizzy from his nearness, but I'm also heartbroken for this burden he's carrying. It was never his. He didn't earn it. It was forced upon him by a father so rotten and evil that he could give Satan a run for his money.

"Alex, I think I know..." I say. His eyes flicker and bounce between both of mine.

"You *don't*," he insists.

But I cut in again with, "I. Do. Know." I swallow the

grit and pain down. I knew then, the moment Alex held me, crying as I cried over my father's death. I knew, but I denied it, because everything hurt me too much.

"Alex you didn't kill my father; you simply didn't save him." Alex's entire body grows tense, and I add, "You wanted to, but you just couldn't."

"Jojo, I'm so sorry." His shoulders sag and his eyes begin to water. I bring his lips to mine and press a kiss against the saltiness, then kiss his head as I pull him into me, cradling him as his arms cling for me.

"I wasn't smart enough...never fast enough. And my father was always one step ahead, playing me—betraying us all. That day, he lured me to the wrong side of the silo; it was like trying to stop a hurricane from hitting land." His body quakes, and I hold him tighter as he clutches me like I'm a life raft.

"I know," I choke out. "I know."

We rock, and with my face hidden from his view, I cry too.

"It was all part of your father's sick scheme. And whatever went down that day, you must know that I forgive you, even though there is nothing to forgive. My dad...what happened and how he died...that wasn't on you."

"But even still, Jojo." His voice is rough—harsh and hurting. "I can't forget it. I can't get the image out of my mind, and I think, because of that, even if you forgive me, I will never be able to forgive myself."

"You must. You were a kid. I was a kid. The feud was

bigger than both of us. But it's over now. It's over, and if you can't move past this, then you and I can never win. Please, Alex. Please. Tell me about that day, because what I've imagined is far worse than the reality. I know it is. Tell me my father's last words."

He shakes his head *no* and my lips press on the top of his head as he shudders out a rough but clear "Okay."

6.

ALEX, JUNIOR YEAR, THE DAY THINGS CHANGED FOREVER.

I nside the granary, Father's voice has reached that inhuman shriek that always scares the shit out of me. Only, inside this closed space it's bigger and monstrous—like an echoing surround-sound theater, bouncing off the walls and slamming cannonballs of hate into each of us.

It's the voice that comes when Father wants to hurt someone. It comes with fists, punches or elbows that blast me, or Grady, and at times even Mother, across a room, into car doors, into pavement or walls. This time, maybe because he can't reach any of us, Father slams the wrench against the granary wall, making us all jump with each reverberating whack.

But then he stops. He seems to calm himself for a long moment. When he speaks again he's transformed from ranting maniac into something much worse. He's grown into this trembling and quiet force. This is the state of being I've learned is scarier than when he's beating us. His voice morphs to match the man. This is the calm before the storm that brings hail and lightning. This is the preface to destruction.

"Mr. Wallace and I have made a new deal today. Haven't we?"

Mr. Wallace nods at my father once, then locks a pleading gaze onto me for a brief yet endless moment.

The gaze says Mr. Wallace is locked in to whatever this "new deal" might be. I think he's promised not to speak, not to fight—not to do anything to upset my father—because, *fuck!* I think he's trying to save *me*.

He wants to save me so I can somehow do the impossible. He's wishing for me to save his Jojo, just as I've promised him I'd do all along.

He knew this day would come.

Can't he see into my eyes the way I can see into his? *I can't do what he wants. I'm afraid and I'm helpless and stupid and there's no way I can protect anyone!* I shout back at him in my stare, keeping my eyes wide and boring into him with every desperate expression I can muster. *I can't save Jojo. I can't save anyone or anything—not you, not me, not her, not anyone. I can't do it!*

I plead more, shaking my head. I plead with him to help me.

Fight. Fight hard. I obviously don't have what it takes. Please, Mr. Wallace. Fight!

Mr. Wallace answers me with the a second, and

nearly imperceptible, head shake and Father, when he sees the silent communication happening between us, holds the wrench up close to the man's face, shoving it up against his forehead, as though he wishes he could crack Mr. Wallace's skull with it.

I wince, waiting for the blows, as does Mr. Wallace.

Surprisingly, that first blow never happens, and when Father walks away to begin loosening the bolts that hold the ramp Mr. Wallace is standing on, Mr. Wallace rips his gaze away from me and lowers his head and sighs, staring down at the sixty-foot depth of grain that will soon swallow him up.

He's waiting for it to be over now.

No! No. No!!

My body begins to hurt from the inside out. My chest aches from holding back my screams. Mr. Wallace's shoulders slump. The sight hurts so badly I can hardly hide my expressions behind the hard mask my face has been morphing into since he turned away from me.

I picture Jojo's face and from there, from deep inside myself, I find the strength to keep it all hidden.

I have to save myself, because I have to save Mr. Wallace's daughter.

Jojo.

Not my Jojo.

Not anymore.

She can never be mine again.

Not after today. Not after this. I'm no longer her 'true-

love' because I'm now a monster. A Sinclair. Like them. But maybe, if I follow all the rules, if I don't rebel this time and I accept what and who I am, maybe I can still be Jojo Wallace's protector. That...that would be enough.

"Boys, take note." Father's chuckling as he shouts out to us. "I've promised Mr. Wallace a whole bunch of shit here today. He and I have our own contract," Father's rantings go on, "and, *unlike you, Alex Sinclair, my fucking shit-excuse for a son,* I'm a man of my word. Yes, I am."

Father flips his head and sears me with a scathing look so hot, heat burns into me, even from this far away.

"I've promised this man that we shall *not* kill his dear Jojo or her mother—not outright—though it would be fun. I've also promised that they will not find a bloody and battered man half buried in a ditch with his face bashed in, which is why I didn't smash in his skull just now."

Father sighs like he's full of regret before turning back to grunt as he works methodically, loosening each of the bolts. They come undone, one by one. He slides them out of the wall carefully. I know these bolts well, and there are only eight holding up the end of the entire walkway that's supporting Mr. Wallace.

Father's now removed six.

Mr. Wallace knows, too.

"I've promised that if he goes quietly, his family will seek solace in the idea that he died in an *accident,* a sad and terrible accident, instead of everyone in Tacoma having to wake up and wonder who in our town is a murderer. A clean death will also keep the grain clean. We'll fish him out all nice and clean, and the Wallaces can eat this winter, too."

Father takes all of the bolts he's unscrewed thus far and drops them all into the grain, letting them sink in. The grain husks puff up into a little cloud of dust as gravity pulls them in slowly and steadily like rocks tossed into quicksand until they disappear. When they're gone, Father pauses again and turns back to me with a point. "Alex, apologize to me, and to Mr. Wallace, like a man. Own this. You fucked up. I'd planned to kill him eventually, but your endless rebellion is why he dies today instead of later. You kept trying to fuck me over, and because of that, you stole from Mr. Wallace. You stole his time."

I take father's direction immediately. "I'm sorry, Father." I respond woodenly, heart falling through my soul and out my feet. It sinks slowly through the three hundred feet of grain inside this metal granary, falling like lead through the earth, all the way through to the blackness that I'm becoming.

"I'm so sorry, Mr. Wallace," I call out loudly. This apology...this one, I mean.

I hope Mr. Wallace can hear it in my voice—see it in my eyes.

I'm so fucking sorry. Sorry...sorry...helpless...

Mr. Wallace flicks me a lightning fast glance, but keeps his head down.

"Stop looking at him, boy. Look at your father!"

Father's voice grows rubber-band taut like he may start shrieking again. "Tell me you're done fighting my will and my plans."

Father's eyes are twin ice stones of cold, cold hate.

"No more, Sir. I'm done fighting your will and your plans. Completely done."

When Father gets the second-to-last bolt out, a deafening creaking and a groaning pierces the air as the entire far end of the walkway that's holding Mr. Wallace bends with a screeching howl as the metal folds downward in this graceful arc.

Father seems surprised by this, as though it was unexpected, and he leaps back onto the portion of the walkway that is secured while Mr. Wallace lunges and grips onto anything he can, shifting his weight to stay on the walkway as the thing moves further down, then pauses, hanging perfectly over the center of the silo's grain storage area. Father's obviously elated at how dramatic everything looks. And Mr. Wallace's eyes show panic for the first time. My eyes rivet on him, and because I know him so well—because he and I are so similar—we're both analyzing if there's a rope or anything at all near, something jutting out of the smooth metal walls of the granary he could maybe swim to or cling to until he could get a breath.

But like me, he knows—there is nothing.

Father and Grady must have removed the safety and rescue ropes each walkway boasted only days ago.

As if it will help, I hold my breath as Mr. Wallace

dangles there, making no sound. I suppose he'd promised my father he wouldn't, but I sense his silence, like mine, is his own type of rebellion, because we both know my father would love it if this would erode into me and Mr. Wallace screaming, begging and crying. We all watch Mr. Wallace's strong hands turn red as he grips the metal.

Strong hands turn red and start to slip.

The place grows so quiet the sound of a cellphone receiving a text startles us. Father pulls Mr. Wallace's iPhone out of his pocket. "Fuck. I nearly walked away with evidence." He makes this tsk-tsk sound as he pauses to read the text.

"Oh...it's your lovely daughter. *Jojo.* Texting from your wife's phone, reporting that she left her phone at school. She and Mom are on the way home. Do you want them to grab you a burrito? The usual? Hmm?"

Father puts the wrench under his arm to blink at Mr. Wallace while he lets out a groan of frustration as he's now trying to climb back up, but his legs fail to hook on, and the walkway groans and dips to a perfect vertical angle.

"I'm going to say that you *do* want one. If I'm hungry, you must be famished." He reads his response out loud as he types. "Yes, honey. Please. If Mom's not too tired. I'm still doing the bolts up in the granary. Almost finished. See you soon."

Father winks at me, and then he flings Mr. Wallace's phone into the wheat. It lights up for a brief moment before it, too, sinks under. As it disappears, the phone dings the text response from Jojo, and Father pouts, adding cruelly, "Do you think she responded, *'I love you, Daddy?'*"

He turns his back on Mr. Wallace then slams the wrench into the last bolt. "Grady, meet me down at the bottom and get my car started. We need to be long out of here when those bitches pull in."

"You want me to just leave Alex here? What if he manages to rescue the guy?"

"Are you questioning me, Grady?" Father asks, his voice all ice and threats for my brother now as the last bolt cracks in half and the metal walkway falls in, bringing Mr. Wallace into the grain with it. "Alex can't get around to this side to help him in time, and he won't anyhow. Because he knows what he's supposed to do this time. Don't you, *Alex?*"

It's not a question. It's a bomb to my heart. A threat to all that I hold dear.

"Yes, sir," I answer him, swallowing down a thousand razorblades. I'm unable to hide the tears streaming down my face as Mr. Wallace stops struggling completely. He told me once that should anyone fall in, struggling only makes the sinking happen faster. "I'll be here. I'll intercept them, and I'll walk with Jojo up here to help search for her father. And then, just as you asked me to, I'll pick up all of the pieces. I'll stand by and watch her and her mother cry, and I'll report it all back to you. Every. Single. Weep."

"Good. You do that. Grady, move your slow ass. Let's go!" Grady leaves me as ordered. And without another word or glance at Mr. Wallace, Father chucks the wrench at the best man I've ever known.

I fall to my knees. The metal walkway has already sunk all the way in, but because it was flat and wide, Mr. Wallace was able to clamber up on it for a time, and that walkway allowed him to sink much slower than the bolts and the phone did.

"Hold on! Can you find a way to hold on?" I'm asking him, though I know it's futile. "I'll go find a rope!"

I stand, knowing better.

"Don't. No time. You know that, Alex. Please stay." Mr. Wallace calls out. "Don't leave me alone. Just look at me. Give me your word that you love my girl—that you will never stop—that you'll love her forever and keep her—" his chin sinks under, and he's spitting wheat grains out of his mouth while adding, "safe. Please!"

"I will. I will never stop."

"I know," he calls back to me, beginning to cough. He's trying to swim up into the grain and onto his back.

I'm sobbing now, reaching towards him under the walkway on my side. My arms are miles from where his body is, where it is now going under. "I love your daughter. I'll never stop loving her. My whole life, I'll work to keep her safe or I'll die trying, sir. I promise. I won't let them hurt her."

"Good. You're good, Alex." I think I hear him say those words, but then he's gasping and coughing as the wheat grains get deeper into his mouth. "It's not your fault, Alex. This is not your fault. My wife...your father. This feud is not your fault. Okay?"

"It is my fault, Sir. I should have known better. Next time I'll see it coming." I shout out above his coughs and his now wild struggles as he begins gasping for the air he can't seem to find anymore. I stay there as he asked, and because I don't know what else to do for him, I say it all again. "I'm sorry. And I promise you, I will love Jojo more than myself. Jojo won't know, and I'll be by her side, and she and your wife—they will be safe. I'll do my best to keep them safe."

"Not your fault. Tell them Alex. *Tell Jojo. Love. Her.*"

He doesn't say more. He can't because he's choking—suffocating—and the last thing I see are Mr. Wallace's eyes boring up at me.

He's anguished.

Afraid to die.

He knows, though, that it's happening. Yet, just like his daughter, he's also somehow forgiving me—even when I don't deserve it.

I won't accept his forgiveness. I should have been able to stop this.

I want to die. I want to fling myself into the grain after him. But I don't—I can't, because I've promised him. Because he just said, "Jojo. Love. Her."

And because I do, because I love her so damn much, I stay where I am. I wait until every last scrap of his blue and green flannel plaid shirt has sunk into the grain, and until I can't hear or see any more movements of struggle under it. It takes longer than it would most men. Mr. Wallace is a fighter, even when there is no hope.

I scream when he's gone, howling my anguish and frustration. I cry out until Jojo and her mother pull up to the farmhouse.

I fly down the steps, shouting for them with my face all swollen from crying and my eyes all desperate with desolation, hurt and pain, and I shake from the horrible shock my body has gone into. They believe me without question as I repeat my father's lies.

"Horrible. Terrible...*accident.*"

7.

ALEX, JUNIOR YEAR. AFTER THE MURDER.

When I'd returned home, it was ten hours since I'd last seen my father.

Ten hours since I'd been a murderer.

Ten hours of hurt.

Father had been waiting for me in his silk bathrobe, smiling maniacally from his success. He's just like a comic book villain. I could hardly look at him, but I made myself do it, and by 4 a.m., I'd reported all he asked of me. Every single blow-by-blow moment, all with a straight face despite my shock, exhaustion and horror that I was still participating like a puppet on a string.

I delved out facts like:

It was Mrs. Wallace who called 911 from her cellphone, right there, while sitting in her car.

She paled and started crying immediately and didn't stop crying the entire night.

Every EMS outlet in the city appeared. Police, fire, ambulances. The newspaper.

It was Mr. Smith, the Tacoma Fire Department Chief, who'd come up with the genius idea to drop a large weighted crane hook into the grain, and because someone had spotted a disturbance in the top layers of the grain, they managed to figure out where Mr. Wallace's dead body might be resting amidst the heavy metal.

It was Officer O'Leary who took my initial statement. He told me I may need to come into the station tomorrow for questioning.

I told them I hadn't seen Mr. Wallace and was looking for him when I noticed the granary door open. I said I couldn't find anyone around the farm. When I went up into the granary, I saw the railing stripped out of the wall and assumed the worst had happened, which is why I was crying and so upset when Jojo and Mrs. Wallace arrived. I told the officer that I had an appointment to help him tighten the walkways this coming weekend, and Mrs. Wallace confirmed it. She told the officer that maybe her husband had tried to fix the railing himself, thinking it would be okay because he'd done it before. She told them that side of the granary had always been a problem.

Mrs. Wallace was so weak from her chemotherapy—

so devastated from this news—that she wasn't able to climb the stairs to see her husband pulled out.

Jojo went in, though. She was there the whole time, crying, letting me hold her.

She nearly crumbled when she told me what I already knew, that she'd been texting him right before it had happened. She blamed herself for distracting her father.

Of course Jojo Wallace would try to take the blame. But it was mine. Mine!

Father loved the part about when they pinged Mr. Wallace's cellphone. I told him we could all could hear it just under the grain. Jojo nearly fainted then, and I had to carry her down the stairs and out to Mrs. Wallace with the help of one of the firemen.

Father made me recount every detail of Jojo and Mrs. Wallace holding the man they loved, dead, in their arms. I told him how they both sobbed when they brought him out. He was still warm, but it was only probably from the grain. Father also loved my description of how, when the EMS guys opened his mouth to try to do CPR, Mr. Wallace's entire airway was so full of pale-yellow wheat grains that his mouth and nostrils looked as though someone had shoved tinted cotton balls into them. Not a single one of the EMS workers could come close to clearing his airways, and that's when Jojo screamed so hard she needed a sedative.

My father reveled in the idea that Jojo was not okay, that the doctor who showed up told me she maybe wouldn't be okay for a very long time after what she'd seen.

I didn't report to Father that I also would not be okay. That I may also need a sedative, and that I wanted to get Father's gun and blow my brains and his brains out right now. Because, obviously, Father wouldn't care about those details, and at this point, I was done being stupid and naive. I well understood that Father enjoyed betraying innocence. Mine—Jojo's—hell, even Grady's. We were just pawns inside his dark and fucked up fun-feud.

My anger and absolute bitterness filled me up that night. It gave me backbone. Through every word, my father smiled, a freakish and very real smile.

He told me how proud he was of me, that I would continue to report to him, and that my work was just beginning. When Jojo broke, her mother broke too. That's how it works—threaten the kids, fuck up the kids, and everyone falls into line. I'd given him exactly what he'd been waiting for. I'm the key to it all. Because of me, every fucking breath Mrs. Wallace draws in, until the day she dies, will burn fire-and-pain inside her heart and head.

Father grinned like a satisfied wolf, or the actual Devil, telling me how happy he was that Mrs. Wallace was smart. He said he knew she would suspect him and his young Sinclair boys. She'd suspect even more that I may have actually killed her husband myself. Then he told me that she would probably expect me to kill Jojo one day, too.

I honestly don't know how I managed to keep my face straight at those horrible words and images. But that's when I knew that I changed. Fully. Inside and out. This had changed me. And, like the man my father wanted me to become, I didn't even blink. I didn't deny the ideas or reject them either. I didn't bother to shout out that he was crazy—that all of this was crazy and that the feud needed to stop because I knew of a better way.

Because I didn't. Not anymore. This was the *only* way, the only way to keep Jojo alive.

I nodded and smiled, copying his expressions and demeanors the best I could, and answered, "Yes, sir. Whatever you want next. And yes, I'll report more tomorrow."

He laughed and tousled my hair like a kid who'd won a soccer match. "So proud of you, boy. Glad to have you ramped in to the future," he said, acting like it was a normal day and I was joining the family business. I guess I was.

He left me with one final chill before he went back to bed.

"May as well stay awake son. I'm sure you can't sleep anyhow. I'll wake the cook and tell her to get you some coffee and food. You've got school today. You better not be missing one class or assignment, either. Your father didn't die last night, after all. You can visit Jojo after school. You can bring her phone to her...you know, when you 'find it at school?'"

He laughed all the way down the hallway.

I slumped into his office chair and the bleary-eyed cook brought me some coffee, her eyes going wide as she saw my face. Though I had no appetite, I washed my face in ice cold water in the office's adjoining bathroom, and ate every bit of the eggs and bacon, telling myself to swallow when all I wanted to do was vomit. I knew I needed my strength to get through the school day so I could get to Jojo's house as soon as possible—as soon as was allowed and commanded by my father.

As all of my tears dried up and I couldn't squeeze out anymore, I watched the sunrise. After an hour of working hard to breathe in and out, I forced myself to relive the vision of Mr. Wallace's face until it became seared on my soul. My father's voice echoed inside my head. I promised myself I'd revisit the memory every single damn day of my fucking worthless life just to make sure I would remember.

As I pushed my plate bitterly across Father's desk, the last shred of what was once me burst forth with an idea. I had one last rebellion.

It was stupid of me, really, because if Father stumbled back in and caught wind of the thoughts in my head and what I was about to do, he would have killed me without hesitation. But at that moment, the core of the old me was warring with the new one.

I wanted to give Jojo something huge, something that

could make it all better, as if I ever could. I wanted her to have something to hold over my father like a dagger too.

I dug out the keys to Father's special cabinet. He kept them in a hidden alcove that was built under his massive wooden desk. Only Mother, Grady and I knew about the keys and the drawer where Father kept his deeds, passports and secrets. This drawer contained everything important to him and his businesses, and he was so organized, so methodical, that I found the deed to the lake easily. The papers for the lake he'd given me were placed in a file folder marked Alex Sinclair Deeds/Trusts/Tax Shelters.

The lake. My lake, so the deed said, though the first time I received it I only glanced at my name on it. I didn't read it like I was reading it now. But back then, three years ago, I was just a kid. Now, I was a man looking at his land trusts and deeds, looking at a way to give one of them away.

Jojo had lost her father today. She didn't know it yet, and maybe she wouldn't have to know it, but she'd also lost her boyfriend. I knew I could never be the same person to her ever again. I could never look at her the same way, or be anything but a fake, horrible liar. But the lake—our lake, which was the only thing left of my heart that was still beautiful and clear and pure—could be saved. It was the only thing that was truly mine. It was mine to give. And I gave it to my Jojo.

I wrote my name in the empty column that said

Transfer of Deed—List Shared Property Holders.
Then I hoped to God that I understood the small print
of the document. I also prayed my Father wouldn't find
out what I'd done for a long, long time. I hoped that
somehow this gesture would give my fucked-up
shredded heart and soul some solace. Glimmers of
redemption. A future for Jojo that one day she could
claim for herself and the life she deserved to have in that
future—*with someone else.*

I printed my name very carefully, and then I signed
my name where directed along with the date. Then I
wrote Jojo Wallace's name, just as carefully. Because we
studied together so much, I knew exactly how she wrote
her letters. Heck, I'd written her name for her many
times already, because Jojo always forgot to put her
name on her assignments. I forged her signature next,
every stroke of pen perfect, right next to mine...where it
would be safe.

I added her address and birthdate to the document,
and after checking the entire deed to be sure I hadn't
missed any spots that may need initials, I stole a stamp
off Father's roll, snagged a proper envelope from his
side drawer, and took the time to look up how and
where to send the document so these changes of property ownership would be recorded inside the State of
Washington Registrar's Offices, as well as within the
County Land Offices.

My only job would be to check the mail every single
day to make sure I intercepted the documents that

would reflect the changes to the deed. That would be easy because Father never got his own mail directly. That was considered menial work. He wouldn't look for this copy of the deed—nor would he suspect it to be missing—and in the off chance he did find it gone, he would assume he'd filed it somewhere else and spend some time looking.

I carefully placed my file folder back in it's proper place, minus my deed to my lake—mine and *Jojo's* lake. I replaced Father's keys, too. And when I went to school that day, I stopped at the post office to make copies and mail everything, keeping the altered original inside the freshly cut lining of my school backpack. I'd even re-sewed it closed.

It took ten days straight of lurking around the mail that was deposited on Father's desk by our maid until I had the new and legal copies of the registered deed also sewn into my schoolbag as well.

Only then did I try to breathe in and out each day. I fought impulses to kill myself and to kill my own father, and I did exactly what he said to protect Jojo from more hurt.

I made myself live as a proper Sinclair.

8.

JOJO, PRESENT DAY.

Bliss this awesome should get to last forever.

This last week has been a stillness of time. I'm not entirely convinced we haven't died or aren't dreaming each and every moment.

This home, this time here with him, has been a sweet afterlife. Something I thought I might never get to have with Alex—and it's also changing into what I hope will be my forever finally coming true.

There isn't a room in this house where we haven't made love. There isn't a part of my body that doesn't ache from our constant touching. I ache for more.

He told me this home was built as a gift for me, that it stood as an architectural reminder for the love we shared. Alex said he built each corner of it to reflect things about me.

My heart expands every time I see something new he put here just for me. Every time he tells me something

ELIOT SCOTT

romantic and sweet and slightly insane—like how he worked so long to get the tiles surrounding the bathtub to match my eyes—I fall in love a little deeper.

This morning, it was the box of my notes and letters that I found stashed between two of his favorite books on the middle shelf in his library. My words and promises to him have been nestled in that cigar box between Tolkien and King since we've been apart. How fitting he stored them in his library.

Our library.

He insists everything here is mine just as much as it's his. I want to trust how genuine it is. The house, him, his words and our resurrection as a couple feels so good, so right, and just how I imagined it would. Only, I just can't seem to let go of that last thread of caution. It's fear and worry, really, that none of this is real.

I cling to the sensation, waiting for the other shoe to drop and one more Sinclair trick to gut me, because that's how I've been trained and conditioned by them. Even from his grave, Mr. Sinclair has us behaving as he'd like—holding back, analyzing each other's every move and word. Even after one week of making love and promises to each other, Alex and I are still scared to death and acting like untrusting and wounded fools who might never come together completely. Like how oil can never, ever mix with water.

Maybe that's why we've been so hungry for each other.

We started this morning just as we have the last four

—making love in the enormous shower that feels like a decadent waterfall cave crested with silver and turquoise jeweled stones.

It started innocently, though we both knew it wouldn't end that way. While I've been the instigator the last two mornings, today it was Alex's turn. He insisted on washing my hair for me, and as I tilted my head back into the warm stream of water to wash away the foaming shampoo, Alex ran his fingers through the long strands bringing the soapy flow of water to my breasts.

With one touch, I was ready. His hands lathered my skin until I was slick everywhere, feeling the contrast of his hands sliding over the raw tips of my breasts until they were completely clean of soap so he could suck them to painfully delicious peaks.

This was the first time he took me this way—from behind. He was gentle at first, his fingers running against my tender skin until I was so swollen and ready that I nearly came in his hands. He turned me so I faced the glass, pressing my breasts flat against it so we could watch each other in the mirror on the other side of the room.

He slid into me slowly, the angle strange but not painful. With each thrust, I grew bolder and my body formed to him this way more until finally he was pounding into me with so much force that I had to steady myself by flexing my arms and spreading my hands out on the glass wall.

I watched him the entire time—his eyes locked on

mine in our reflection as his face grew rigid with want and need. He took me—possessed me—and the power of his stare was so fucking seductive. Long gone are the days of innocent exploration of our bodies by the water under the trees. This man, his abs a sculpture of perfection that curve into his loins, and his arms dented where they should be and defined by discipline, is mine to touch and to taste, and I will have him.

My body is now sore from Alex, the bruising and scrapes from Grady nearly healed. We may need to spend the day doing something mundane and domestic, as my insides are raw from his thick cock. Even this morning I had to pull him out of me before he finished, dropping to my knees in the shower and stroking him until he came on my breasts.

Honestly, I would be satisfied lying like this, in his arms, on this sofa that overlooks the still water outside.

"Maybe we should take you shopping to get some clothes...not that I don't love how you look in my white T-shirts and sweatpants."

I turn into Alex and he kisses the end of my nose.

"I told my aunt I would be by her place later to gather my things." I've been texting her daily so she doesn't worry, but I think if I don't come back to her place soon she'll start to suspect that I'm secretly in trouble and being forced to tell her I'm fine.

I am fine, though. I've never been so fine. And that's part of the reason I have been so hesitant to leave this safe space—this moment. I don't know if I'll ever get it back. My body tingles with the millions of questions that race through my head from here. I don't know if I come back to Alex's house after I see my aunt, or if I go back to Ohio to get Emily. I don't know if I bring her to Alex first, or if I tell him about her and take her to him. I don't know if this is how we do this—or if we run away.

There's also the incessant worry of whether or not we're truly safe. This game, it's gone on for so long it's hard to be certain that I'm not still in the thick of it. If this is a plot, how can I risk bringing Emily into it. I wear that worry, and Alex massages the small dent it makes on my forehead.

"Grady won't hurt you again," he says, assuring me.

I smile with tight lips and wiggle into his chest.

"I know." I breathe in deep and hold my lungs full, trying not to think of that other lingering question. It's there, though; it's always going to be there until it's cleared from both of our heads.

"Alex?" My voice is raspy with lack of sleep, and I debate whether to ask him now or to just fall asleep with the breeze spilling in through the window.

"Mmmm hmmm." His chest vibrates against my jaw. His smell fills me up. He can feel me tremble. I know he can.

"Jo, ask me. Tell me. Leave nothing unknown. That's what we pledged, and you have to let go of it. What is it?" He twists and dips his chin into his chest as his thumb lifts mine until our eyes meet.

I practice the words in my head six or seven times before they finally leave my lips.

"Did you kill your father?"

I'm not sure what to expect, but the laughter that comes after long seconds of complete silence lets me breathe.

"Jo...oh god, no. No. I mean...I wanted to, yes." He shakes his head then lifts me as we both sit up, and he pulls my legs over his lap leaving enough distance to look directly into my eyes. "No, Jojo. I didn't murder my father. And I'm guessing since you asked that..."

He shrugs and it takes me a few seconds to catch on. When I do, I burst out a short laugh and cup my mouth.

"You thought..." My eyes are wide in surprise. I'm almost a little proud that Alex thinks I'm capable of murdering his dad, as sick and twisted as that is.

"Not really, but I wondered a little maybe, deep in the back of my mind. You had plenty of reasons to do it, and I'm pretty sure there's a list of people in town who would lie to give you an alibi." Alex runs his thumb over my brow and follows the trail of his hand down my face with his eyes.

"I guess the suspect list in this town is pretty long," I say.

Alex nods.

Our peace is suddenly interrupted by the familiar song blaring from somewhere in the kitchen. I recognize it instantly, but somehow I have the strength to wear the mask. It's Emily's favorite Taylor Swift song, but I act as if I have no idea who could be calling. I pull back slightly and Alex draws his brow in and bunches his lips in a tight smile.

"That's an interesting ring tone," he says through a chuckle.

I hold the smile in it's place, but my heart beats once in a heavy thud that drains the blood from my arms and legs. I stumble as I climb from Alex's lap and try to steady myself as I rush to the counter. I don't realize he's followed me until I find the buzzing, blinking and pop-tune blaring phone at the very bottom of my purse.

"Emily...Emily..." Her name comes out in a panic, afraid I missed her call, and when I look up, Alex is sitting on the wooden stool at the kitchen island only inches away from me.

"Mommy!" She shrieks my name excitedly, like she always does when we haven't talked for a few days, and all I can think is how I should turn the volume down, how I'm sure Alex heard that word—*mommy*.

I blink, concentrating on the way my mouth rests, willing it to smile but not too much, reminding me to speak in riddles, to keep my voice adult-like.

To lie.

Only finally, after so very long, Alex and I have started telling the truth. I can't go back to deception now. This is the test. It was always going to be the test. Only...I'm so not ready.

Deep breath.

"Hey, I'm sorry I'm winded. I had to rush to the

phone." I flinch when I feel Alex's fingers brush against mine. His brow lowers and his mouth draws in on one side, so I lean forward and kiss his cheek quickly before holding up a finger and stepping away a few paces. As if I could ever walk away enough to make this lie feel right.

"Uncle Jeff needs to talk to you. He got a job offer. In a big *city!*"

My stomach somehow finds new depth, sinking more. Jeff is my rock, and the only safe place for me to run—for me to keep Emily until it's time. He can't move to the city. Especially not this one. And not now.

"Oh, that's exciting. I'd love to hear more. Can you put Jeff on speaker?" I turn and smile in Alex's direction in case he's watching me. I'm relieved that he's not. He's moving around the kitchen now, opening a cupboard and pulling out cups for coffee.

"Hey, Jojo." My best friend has never been good at lying, and I can tell by the hesitation to say anymore, by the way his tone oozes worry and longing and near desperation, that this job offer is something he needs to take.

"Sounds like this is the one, huh?" I'm careful with my words still, even though it's Jeff I'm speaking to.

His sigh is weighted. "It's pretty much perfect, Jo. It's product development and innovation, and I'd be the team lead. I'd basically be in charge of making things that can cure cancer. I can't…"

"I know," I interrupt, my voice hoarse because Jeff is

right—it's perfect. I want him doing work like this. The world needs it as much as my mom's memory deserves it. "You have to."

"It's in San Francisco. And the pay is just…"

"Yeah…" I say.

My resolve falls just enough to let my disappointment show, and Alex's hand is reaching for mine again. I don't flinch this time, instead focusing on the way his hand holds mine as he lifts it to his mouth and presses his lips against my knuckles.

"When do you start?" I ask, locking eyes with Alex before tearing my gaze away from his because I suddenly feel so guilty for not telling him about Emily yet.

"That's the thing…uh…" The other end of the line is silent for a few seconds before Emily breaks in.

"He signs papers today!" My little girl's voice paints the world with her enthusiasm and pride, but it's more than her being happy for Jeff. She knows that means she and I will be together again soon…today maybe!

"Oh. Today? So then you must be in California?" I scratch at my head, trying to find a way to talk in code and digest the avalanche I can no longer stop. The biggest secret of all can't be kept from Alex any longer.

"We're in the driveway. All of us."

Oh, God!

"Yes. Sorry, Jojo. I know you wanted time, but, we're in the driveway. So…I hope you're both dressed."

My aunt is half her usual dry-sarcasm, half apologetic.

My mind starts spinning with the news: *Emily's here. She's in the driveway. Oh God, please help me through this. Please...*

"What?" I choke and all of the air disappears from my lungs as I bring my other hand to the bridge of my nose and squeeze, trying to stop the panic. I can't though. It's rushing in like a flood.

"I'm so sorry, Jojo," Jeff says. "I've got about twenty minutes before I need to hightail it to the airport."

"We've been trying to call." My aunt pipes in next. "May Sinclair has been at the antique shop all morning. She's just hovering around the corner in her car. She even came in and pretended to shop. It's like she knows. I waited until lunch. Flipped the BE BACK IN AN HOUR sign on the door and had to shake her following me. Made it just in time to meet Jeff at the highway junction. The only thing I could think to do was come here. Walt's gone hunting for the next three weeks, and I just don't like the idea of Emily and me being there—that close to May—alone."

Like Jeff, my aunt sounds worried, but I can tell she's also anticipating this—that she's somehow relieved. She's never loved the idea of me keeping this secret, even though she understood why I wanted to wait. And now...I'm thinking maybe she did know best. If May's been at the antique shop, it's probably because I never turned up back at the shop. Or maybe she knows about

Emily? And if that's the case, having her here, between me and Alex, is the safest place she can be. My heart drops with some heavy layers of fear as I let myself wonder the worst case scenario.

What if Alex doesn't want her?

"Well, it's time to rip the BandAid off, I guess." My gaze shifts to Alex's who's approached to set a mug of coffee down next to me. I can't hide my anxiety about this. He's trying to read my mind, just like he always did, and I guess still does. His brow wrinkles with concern.

"What?" he mouths while I try to send out the message—the outcome that I'm now praying for that *all is okay.*

Not a day has passed that I didn't want Emily to meet her daddy, that I didn't want to introduce the two most important people in my life to one another.

It's time; whether I'm ready or not. "People are outside. My aunt and...my roommate Jeff and—" Losing my nerve, I leave off *Emily*, and simply add, "You need to meet them. I'm sorry that it's kind of a surprise. Is it okay if we're invaded?"

"Hell yes," he says, picking up my hand. "Of course."

"Come on in," I say, the words vibrating on a tremor that's half terror and all excitement on their way out.

I intertwine Alex's fingers with my own, kneading our hands together nervously, staring at his skin against mine for just a little longer before I test the bonds of trust that we've only begun to mend.

The line jostles as Jeff switches from speaker, bringing the phone to his ear.

"Jo. I'm so sorry. If this is not okay—if this is too sudden—I can talk them out of doing this now. I can postpone everything."

His offer is actually genuine, and I mentally zoom through the dozens of things Jeff has given up since taking me in as a roommate.

His last boyfriend, who wanted the two of them to move in together, I know why it didn't work out—because of me...and Emily. The last job offer, to teach at UC Davis, wasn't the right fit because it wouldn't be good for me and Emily. And the millions of tiny sacrifices that have happened over the years, like the nights I cried over my fucked-up life and Jeff rocked me to sleep even though he had to work at four in the morning.

"You have to take this. Come in, meet Alex, and then get to the airport."

I pause and stare into Alex's eyes.

"We'll be okay, Jeff. All of us."

"Heading up the steps then. I need to use the restroom," my aunt butts in, and I blink as the line goes dead.

"I never expected you to wait for me, Jojo. I always just hoped you would be happy. And I know you said there wasn't a *someone*, but that...it kinda sounded like a guy *someone*, and from the way you spoke to him, I can tell you love him, and...what am I trying to say? I guess just tell me if you're going to throw yourself at him and kiss him and say something like, '*Hey, honey, I missed you.*' I'll prepare myself for it." His voice cracks. "I need to know so I can prepare my head."

His mouth settles in a tight line, his nostrils flaring with a quick breath as I mentally catch up to what he's thinking.

Oh god...

"No. Alex—you're misunderstanding. It—Jeff—he is someone special but it's not like that between us. You'll see." My throat is scratchy, like sand paper, and every swallow only closes the airway more. I want to shout out that he's got a daughter, that she's on the front porch, but I've lost my courage—and the ability to speak. My insides sink seeing how sad his face looked just now while asking me if he and I are not going to be anything beyond this amazing few days we've shared.

I gather some thoughts and spit them out fast. "I've been living with Jeff while I work and go to college," I start. "But, he...*we*...oh, God," is all that falls out of my mouth.

Again Alex takes them all wrong. "Wow, that's... that's a long time to be dating someone...okay...okay." He pulls in a breath.

"No. Alex!" I put my palm flat against his chest and take a deep breath, hoping a little courage will work its way in along with the air. "We're not together, not at all...*ever*. Not like that. He helps me out tremendously, and I love him, and he loves me, but it's about something else—*something huge.*"

The knocking begins, and I start to lead him toward the doorway. "Just open the door. You'll see, just please...keep a straight face if you can. Please."

"Helps you with *what?*" Alex answers absently as regret flickers across his warm brown eyes. I think he doesn't believe me about Jeff, but he ratchets on his stoic-faced mask as he adds, "And...I was born keeping a straight face on..."

His eyes flit to the door, now rattling with pounding and echoing with incessant dinging. My aunt. *Emily.*

"Jeff. He helps with my...my daughter." I whisper, scooting in front of him, shoving my back against the front door as I hold up my hands, blocking him from opening it. "That's—she's the huge thing."

Alex's whole face has contorted at my words, and his body has grown rigid. His pupils swell, and I know he no longer sees me. He's got this fight-or-flight expression on right now, but he's holding steady because I think his heart knows.

Please, God, let him see into me. Let him see what I'm trying to say.

In case God isn't listening to my prayers—because he's got a habit of ignoring me big-time when I'm in Tacoma— for Emily's sake, I have to add the truth. I have to get it out, and it's going to be the hardest thing I've ever done in my entire life. This truth is so big and scary, but it's so amazing.

I have to believe.

"This isn't how I wanted any of this to happen. And

I'm so sorry that this is how it is—that this is how you're finding out. But I needed to know; I had to be sure. I needed to feel safe. I had a plan, and this sped everything up. I've really messed this up, but Alex…please." I stutter out, letting myself get pulled into what I think is his wide-open, terrified expression. I rush on before I lose my nerve.

"Whatever happens, whatever or wherever your mind goes with this, please forgive me for not knowing how to tell you. She's nearly six, but still five until the end of next month. It mean's she's really little still, but she's so smart."

I breathe, and my lips part before the whisper escapes while my eyes are locked on his.

"Like you."

My voice cracks as I let my fear, my love for our daughter, and everything that makes me into an over-protective mother show on my face.

"She's so sweet, and her imagination is magical. And she's been obsessed with meeting her real father —*you*—for years. I've told her about you since she first asked me about her daddy, so try to be gentle. If you don't want…*us*…that's fine too. Just meet her but spare her, and we will go somewhere and find a way to be happy."

That last part is a lie, but I felt compelled to give him the out. I blink, pleading and dying a little inside. "Okay?"

His eyes hold steady on mine, and that mask he

wears so well shifts into something different—something new.

"Don't say those words, that you'll leave, to me ever again, Jo. No matter what; never again." His eyes slant just a little as tears threaten to form.

"You have to get that idea out of your head—that I won't want you...*or this.* Jo...I won't live another day without you, and, Christ, we have a daughter. We're a family? I'm a father?" The last words slip out in a shocked-sounding whisper. A tear slips down my cheek as I nod my response.

"Just tell me," he goes on. *"Shit.* My legs are shaking so hard right now. And I can't even think straight." A nervous laugh slips out, but he chokes on it quickly. His face has gone completely pale, and he's now running his hands deep into his hair, keeping his thumbs against his temples as though his skull is threatening to blow up.

"Tell you what?" I look up at him, realizing my whole body is shaking as much as his is.

"Just tell me her *name.*" He grabs me by the shoulders, kisses me quickly on my forehead, and gently pulls me off the door while reaching for the handle. "What's her name, so I can say it to her."

"Emily. Her name's Emily. And you are going to love her. I promise."

"More than the sun, Jojo. More than the sun." His voice is sandpaper-rough as he looks back at me, and his beautiful eyes reflect an expression I've never seen before. The fear is gone, and all I can read in there is his wonder and this flash of beautiful trust at what's happening right now.

I swear I also feel something akin to joy seeping into his body, but because he's Alex, and I know him too well, he also can't hide the worry that holds him back. For once, I'm like him—I'm worried, too.

I suck in my breath, hold it tight and pray like I've never prayed before as the man I love so much it hurts pulls the door open wide and looks down at our daughter for the first time.

9.

ALEX, PRESENT DAY.

T he little girl—*Emily*—is smaller than what I'd already imagined *almost-six* might look like. Before I can even focus on her, this voice, clear as a bell, chimes out and sears into my heart. "Mommy! *Mommy!*" she shouts before hurtling herself into Jojo's arms and then burying her face and laughter into her mom's chest.

And just like that, she's inside my house—part of my soul—and my head is spinning so hard as I try to pinch myself awake in case this is some sort of a dream.

My daughter...my daughter.

At twenty-four, I'm too young to be a father...aren't I?

I register that Jojo's Aunt Shelly, and the man named Jeff that Jojo has spoken of so much, have entered into the foyer behind Emily, but it's all in a fog because I can't stop staring. I can't stop the head spinning.

My daughter...my daughter.

Jojo's kneeling, laughing along with her child—fuck...our child—and she's placing her hands all over Emily's face, her arms, her hair, then stroking the little girl's back and shoulders as though she's taking stock of every inch of the little girl.

Emily. Her name is Emily. She's so tiny. So sweet.

Jojo's daughter... Jojo's daughter. Our daughter?

Emily.

Jojo had a baby—our baby—when she was barely eighteen! How...how could she have done this all alone?

Why didn't she tell me right away? Why...?

You know why. Jojo was afraid...probably protecting her child.

Holy...shit!

I've tracked the utter relief and happiness on Jojo's face, and I've deleted all of the *impossibility arguments* that came into my head at first, because Jojo never lies. Never. And she'd never lie about something as huge as this. It feels so unreal, yet here she is in front of me. Emily. Hugging the woman I love. My daughter. Our daughter. A fully formed, yet miniature, whole human being that has lived almost six years.

One whom I didn't even know about a few moments before.

My breathing catches on these last thoughts as my eyes stick onto her profile.

God, she's beautiful, and as shining as a sunbeam hitting the lake. Her laughter's as bright as the moon and sparkles tinkling into the air—*and damn*—but she's so tiny she's all but disappeared again into Jojo's embrace.

As they stay there rocking together, because it's obvious they've missed each other terribly and that they need this time, I can hardly tell where the little girl's long brown, waving hair begins and her mother's beautiful hair ends.

My mind explodes at this realization, that there could be a person with the exact same colors and curls to her hair as Jojo.

They're one and the same...mother, and daughter...and... and...God help my heart. They're both really mine.

My chest twists, my heart pounding so loudly it's like thundering horses. I still can't tear my eyes off of her, nor do I hear one word tumbling out of anyone's mouth.

I have a family. I. Am. A. Father.

How the hell am I ever going to protect her?

I focus in on this new kind of *father-heartbeat* pounding into my chest. It's bigger than me. It's fierce and suddenly it's all consuming, yet oddly it feels like a pounding I've known for my entire life. I find that I'm humbled, empowered and in awe all at once as I breathe in then out, embracing this new consciousness, becoming this new kind of person.

Jojo and I—on the night we gave each other everything—on the night that broke us both—created a symbol of what we truly were to each other. Because we were so very much in love, that's what Emily is to me now, surprising, but pure, and so beautiful. She's innocence and happiness—and absolute love. Our love.

The force of the realization drops me to my knees, and I push away my thoughts of the past and keep them nestled in my growing joy. It's easy to dial into the waterfall of sound that is Emily's perfect, giggling laughter. She's filling up my house with wonder and light, and God, but this past week with Jojo in my house, and in my bed, had me wondering if I could approach her about being really and truly together again. Emily has me solidified. This child has me believing in a power much bigger than any of us.

Her laughter has me believing that our future might be what Jojo has always said it would be despite everything trying to tear us apart. Together, we get to be *good*, and *redeemable*, and *sane*, even after everything. Looking at this lovely sweet child who has her entire future ahead of her, with me and Jojo to raise her...*hell*. I wonder, how could Jojo not be right? How could we not be all of those things if we made this little human together? If God let us have her, we cannot be bad.

When Emily finally turns to face me, I'm blown away, because I'm looking into my own, large, almond-shaped, bright brown eyes. Eyes that are nestled inside of Jojo's delicate, heart shaped face. Emily's long, gangly limbs hint that one day she'll be tall. She's got her arms confidently and possessively draped around Jojo's neck, her fingers are tangled into her mother's hair, and she's leaning her slight weight onto her smiling mom.

I'm so tongue-tied, I can only utter a lame and half-choked-out "Why, hello there...Emily."

"Hello."

She's blinking as though she's a little bit shy all of a sudden, but she holds my gaze. I love how her expression is calm, assured, and that she seems so happy, not just to see her mother, but to see me!

"Do you know who I am?" she asks me, head tilting to the side. She's waiting.

I nod. "You're my daughter," I answer, afraid to move or startle her, or say the wrong things.

"Yes." She nods back, as though satisfied with my answer. "I've been waiting a long time to meet you, Daddy. Do you know that?"

She looks me over, up and down, and then locks back onto my face, studying me sharply and missing nothing.

"I—I—I'm—I—" I stutter at first as I share a quick glance with Jojo, who looks like she's working hard not to hold her breath, and I smile at her, sending what I hope is the message that I'm all in.

Dying, but all in.

I'm sure Jojo's intuitive enough to know that Emily's just imploded and simultaneously claimed my heart forever by simply calling me *"Daddy"* like it's the most normal thing in the world for her to say.

"I'm very sorry you had to wait, Emily." I manage to get my thoughts together. "Sorry that it took way too long for us to meet."

"Me too."

"Can you—" My voice trips, and catches. I feel tears surge at the edges of my eyes, because I've only just met this girl, and I'm suddenly broken and desolate over all of the years I missed. "Can you ever forgive me?"

The numbers play fast, over and over inside my head —*one, two, three, four...five. Nearly six.*

"Yes. I will. If you come to my birthday party and if you stay with us now." Emily commands, immediately forgiving me. My heart twists even more recognizing the no-nonsense voice that comes out of her mouth. It's exactly like Jojo's. And from the look on the child's face, her love is completely the same too.

Open. Trusting. Generous.

Unconditional.

True.

"I will." I answer, honestly, because even the end of the world or an instant ice-age couldn't keep me away from my daughter's birthday party or her from this day forward.

"Mommy said we had the same eyes." Emily leans closer to me. "And..." she points at my face, scrunching up her face hard. "I've seen so many pictures of you, but I didn't really believe her."

She pauses, blinking while she studies me. "But I think it's true. We both do have the same kind of brown color. Did you know that I had brown eyes like yours?"

I don't answer that. It makes me too sad that I didn't know, and I'm not going to lie to her and pretend.

"Brown mixed with real, live gold, and *so*-so *beautiful*." Jojo fills in the words I can't say with her own words. "Emily, your eyes and your daddy's eyes are my favorite eyes. The best eyes. On the best two people. Father-daughter eyes."

"You always say that." Emily laughs then, and parrots, "The famous father-daughter eyes. I used to want green ones like Uncle Jeff's eyes because they're so pretty." Emily points at Jeff, who is a tall, slender man. I've finally been able to acknowledge his presence with a nod and a smile. He's been openly crying and wiping away his tears this whole time. He does have very pretty green eyes, and to me, he appears to be kind, as well as concerned about Jojo and Emily. And I think, maybe also...gay? Please be gay.

Emily continues. "Jeff also told me my eyes are special because they make mommy happy. These eyes." She points at her own face, grinning. "These make her think of you, and Mommy loves thinking about you, Daddy. Jeff and I, we wear matching necklaces now." She pulls out the gold chain she's wearing around her neck and shows me the tiny rose pendant hanging there. "See? It's a rose. Because Uncle Jeff says I'm his little rose. All the time he calls me that. It's my best thing, and he says his necklace is his best thing. That he's never, ever going to take it off of his neck. Right, Uncle Jeff."

"Right. Especially now that I'm going to miss you, *moppet*. Who shall help me choose my outfits every day?"

Jeff pulls out his own pendant and waves it at her, nodding and dabbing at his eyes more.

"Don't cry, Uncle Jeff. Remember? We talked about this. I will FaceTime you every single day. And I will visit you soon, and you will visit me soon."

"I know." Jeff sighs out heavily. "Good that you reminded me."

Emily laughs as though delighted to be the one who's teaching me about her world and tosses me a very knowing look. "My Uncle Jeff cries about everything. Even at TV commercials and all of the Disney movies. And he *always* needs reminders about things."

"Don't out me too much, Emily." Jeff laughs and then dissolves into more tears as Emily runs to fling herself at him.

Jojo laughs and joins Emily in a three-way hug. "Better that Alex knows this about you sooner than later."

Jeff and I exchange a long look, and I can tell the guy is relaxing, trusting me. Trusting the expressions on Jojo's face. Trusting that I'm not going to hurt his little family.

Emily skips out of the hug and over to me, beaming. "That way our new, bigger family will be ready and always have tissues ready for you when you come visit. Right, Daddy?"

"Right," I say, gazing down into Emily's face, feeling suddenly overwhelmed by all of this. I'm freaking out again at my similarities to this child. As much Emily at first appeared to be Jojo's twin—heart-shaped face, fly-away curls and hair color, laughter, smile, freckles, openness, boldness—the eyes are mine. The longer, more stubborn line of her chin, that's mine, too.

Maybe—the stupid impulse to trust in your father—to trust that he loves you—maybe that is also mine...

Staring at her upturned face, I get this sensation that I'm looking into a mirror, and I start to panic.

I suddenly see too much of myself in her eyes. I see my mother, too. And that is something I don't want to see. I don't want this child to have to claim any of that.

My father always made fun of my brown eyes, and for years, I used to hate them. Mother once told me to *never* bring attention to them. It was like she wanted me to never mention how she and I were the same. Father used to call the eyes out whenever I cried, saying that they made me weak. He would tell me not to look at him. And of course, he'd say the eyes were more proof that I was not of *true Sinclair stock*. Grady once told me that Father had beaten Mother for passing my ugly, shit-colored eyes on to me instead of the ice-blue ones he and Father shared.

Back then, I didn't believe Grady. Back then, Grady was the source of all stupidity and lies. He was an unbelievable jealous idiot who wanted Father to like him more than me. I didn't know I was the stupid one. But, by the end of high school, I believed Grady. I believed him about everything, and after Father beat me and broke Grady's throwing shoulder...after he killed Mr. Wallace...I believed it all even more.

Suddenly, it's difficult not to hear voices in my head —my father, my mother, and even my brother. It's even more difficult to not feel completely terrified. Not because I'm an instant-parent, which is terrifying enough all on it's own, but because of my family, and mostly because this poor child has me fucked-up. She has forever ruined me.

I know if my father was alive to see this little girl, he would have hated her. He would have harmed her as quickly as possible. Emily would be Father's worst nightmare. This massive surge of protectiveness slams into me like the fists to my gut my father used to lay on me whenever he caught me off guard.

I take all of it—the pain, the white-hot fear, and the overwhelming love—hard and fast. It's so intense that my shaking legs give out completely. I drop to my knees in front of Jojo and Emily. And far behind my smile that I'm holding in place for Emily, I pray.

I pray that Jojo's love for all of us is enough to heal this madness that licks at my soul. I pray for strength, and that I'm able to be the kind of father this little girl deserves. I pray that I can make every bit of the time we've lost as a family up to Jojo and Emily, somehow.

Most of all, I pray that I can keep my past—my father and his voice—out of my head.

Looking at Jojo's patient smile while the seconds tick by makes it seem easier. Looking into Emily's curious expression—one that is just for me, and just as sweet as Jojo's—I'm able to push back my father's darkness. Already, I'm formulating a plan of what I'm going to do next.

I seek solace and peace in the images of me standing in the Tacoma Cemetery. I replay over and over again how I was the first to shovel the wet earth onto my father's grave, and how Grady was the second.

It's over...this feud, it's over. All I have to do is reconcile with my brother. I'll give him what he wants. The business...fuck, I'll even give him my penthouse and the building that goes with it.

Father's dead. I have no reason to stay here, and every reason to get my family the fuck out of this damn town. We can close up this house. And of course, she and I will keep the lake. But until Emily's all grown up, and the sickness of the feud washes away, we will walk away together, the three of us. I glance at Aunt Shelly and Jeff and change my number to *the five of us*, and we'll never look back.

10.

JOJO, PRESENT DAY.

I think I've gained seven pounds on cookies so far.

It started a week ago, when I drove Jeff to the airport and came back home to find Alex, Aunt Shelly and Emily cooking in the kitchen together. Emily was pouring chocolate chips in slowly while Alex stirred, and as soon as I walked in, they insisted I help them test the dough.

We ate nearly half the bowl before baking the rest of the cookies. We took them out to where the flat rock juts over the lake, and we ate the remainder of the entire pan out there.

It's become a routine, every day, right after lunch.

Alex insists on it, and there's something in the way he sits back and watches sometimes, stares as Emily and I sing our songs while we bake, just as we've always done, that sits warm in my soul.

I didn't understand until yesterday, when he made

the cookies for us early and invited us all out to eat them on the rock. These cookies are a symbol of time for him. Time lost—like the times Alex and I sat on this rock eating the warm baked cookies from his bag long ago. He says it's healing him, making him whole again. So, fine. I will grow fat and happy on these cookies, eating them every day, if it will keep Alex smiling like he's been smiling since we moved Emily and Shelly into this house.

He whistles now, something he's never done. I caught him whistling while he showed Emily how to tie a lure on her line. Our daughter tried to whistle just like her father, but a missing front tooth made it impossible for her. The very next day, he went into town and bought her a small whistle that he said she could use until her tooth came in.

I knew he would love her this much.

Alex was restless last night. I think it's the worry that comes along with being a father. He told me this is what's the hardest for him. It's the hardest part for every parent. I've had nearly six years to get used to that feeling. It's one that is very much tangled up into how I love Emily, and one I think will be part of me forever. I tell him he'll get used to the feeling, that it will fade into this dull ache that defines him now as a parent, but I suppose when you're a Sinclair, your instincts are heightened.

Last night, he shook me awake and took off his tough-guy mask. He shared his worries with me, and let me be a part of them and the solution, finally.

"I want to give Grady everything. The business. My building in town. Hell, even this house, if that's what it takes to end this feud. Grady's been MIA since I beat him into the dirt. He's going to be so fucking pissed off, and I'm worried he's working on some retaliation scheme. That's his way. It's all he knows. I'm going to have to give it all away, Jojo. Whatever he wants. I want my brother to feel like I've lost and he's won. Are you going to be okay with that?" His words came out desperate.

I protested at first, because Alex is the one who deserves everything. His father thought so too, though for different reasons. It's Alex's name was on the will. He's the only one who will turn the Sinclair name into something people no longer fear or look at with disgust.

"Under Grady's control, this company and everything that's ever been a Sinclair will just become uglier, darker, and, if possible, more corrupt," I said.

"I don't care, Jojo. I want to walk away from here. We'll be nearly destitute, but we can start over. Will you —can you imagine doing that with me, and with Emily?"

I kissed him. "It was never about the wealth for me, Alex. You know that. I just loved the boy."

I kissed him again. "And now I love the man, as does Emily. It's a good idea."

"It's a *great* idea. God…how I love you, Jojo. I can't believe I get to have this second chance with you. This family. We could end up living in a tent, you know."

"We won't, Alex. I've got a good job. I'll take care of you."

He'd blinked down at me, shaking his head while I ran a finger up and over his beautiful smile, before going on. "Besides, we're going to need a two-bedroom tent...so we can..."

Alex didn't let me finish that line.

He kissed me back, hard, his hands already pushing up my white camisole and stripping it off so my breasts were bare for his eyes to see. My body squirmed under him, my hands worked to push down and kick off my panties, then helped him out of his boxers.

We went with zero foreplay this time. The way his eyes looked—the way he looked at me, so open and bare —I wanted him inside of me. I guided him there, both of us urgent and pulsing and pushing and pounding.

My legs locked tightly around his waist, my body arched up and into him and we were like waves crashing on a beach, over and over again. Our breathing was in sync, matching as we grew faster, and faster, until we came at the same time, both of us surprised and panting. We lay there whisper-laughing against each other's necks until Alex's body relaxed into my arms. Seconds later, he fell into a deep sleep.

I suppose our lovemaking momentarily took the worries away from him and transferred them into me, adding to my own guilt over what Alex had done to defend me by nearly killing Grady, and by what he now had promised to give away to make it right. He was promising it all to make me and Emily—his family —safe.

I barely slept, and when I woke up after finally getting to sleep as the sun rose, that sense of responsibility was still there. It wasn't just about Alex though, it was a guilt about social responsibility. We can't trade our own peace of mind for something that will give Grady permission to continue to destroy the place we've both called home for years. Grady is going to drain the water out of these lands, and then go for the oil, destroying of every bit of the environment here so he can gain more of what he does not need. Money.

Unfortunately, I think Alex is right. Leaving here is the only way to stop the bitter feud, but maybe Alex and I can come up with a way for us to hang on to something—*something* that we can use later as leverage. But we can't do that until we're all safe and thinking clearly.

Alex left early this morning to get Emily an "important thing." He said it while rolling out of bed just as I was finally finding slumber. He's been gone for hours now, and that uneasy feeling is starting to chip away at my nerves—my imagination. Did he already try to approach Grady...or is he with his attorneys, trying to come up with the paperwork he's going to need to hand it all over to his brother? Or is he really out "getting something for Emily?"

Aunt Shelly isn't helping, either. She won't come out and ask me where he is; probably because she knows I

don't know. She also won't directly voice her suspicions
—that Alex is being played, or worse, playing us.

Is he with May, his mother? That would make the
most sense considering how she's been lurking around.

*Is this is a trap and we're just sitting here, like open
targets.*

Shelly won't say it with her voice, but her expression
is enough. She's been pretending to read on the sofa for
an hour, bending the newspaper forward every few
minutes and sliding her glasses down her nose to glance
at me with a raised brow. I, in turn, pretend I don't see it
every time, but the second she raises the paper again, I
stare at her with a force that might just burn through
that front page soon.

"Bananas are on sale," she finally says.

"I love those!" Emily shouts from the seat across the
table from me. She leaps from her chair and crawls onto
the sofa with Aunt Shelly, snuggling in to look at
pictures in the paper with her. It's actually been nice
having my aunt here. With Walt gone for his annual
hunting trip, she hasn't felt safe staying at the antique
shop alone.

"Don't show her the bad stories," I say. I'd rather give
my daughter innocence when I can, and I know how my
aunt likes to direct the news.

"We're looking at the food ads." Aunt Shelly waves
her hand in my direction.

I step up and glance at the pages in her hand to make

sure she's not lying, and I'm relieved when I see the poultry and bread photos on the page as she turns it.

"Daddy's home!" Emily announces, pushing hard from her aunt's belly, using enough force to make Shelly grunt.

"How do you know?" I stand and work my hands into my pockets so no one can see how I've been nervously picking at my fingers for hours.

"The lights reflect on the ceiling when he pulls in the driveway! I wait for them." She starts to bounce on her toes about a dozen feet away from the front door, and I hear the car door slam outside. I smirk and think of how observant my girl is. Those skills will serve her well.

The door cracks open at first, and I stand behind Emily and meet Alex's gaze.

"Hey." His smile is crooked. Guilty?

"Hey." I frown, pulling my brow in, noticing he's clearly hiding something behind the door.

"I'm sorry I was gone so long. My phone died, and I didn't have my charging cable. My hands were a little full, too." The smile on his face grows tighter, so tight that I start to mimic it.

Something is up. What's wrong?

"Alex?" My pulse is kicking at my insides with hesitant anticipation.

"Don't be mad," he says quickly, his arm finally giving way as a golden, curly-haired puppy gently falls to the ground and cautiously ambles across the marble and onto the wood-planked floor into the arms of our squealing daughter.

"You got a puppy!" Emily shrieks, falling on her butt and then lying down as the pup crawls over her belly and begins licking her chin. Her giggle shakes her chest and she works to roll with the puppy and cling to him with the grip of an Olympic wrestler.

"Alex, oh my!" My mouth hangs open in awe at the sight of Emily and this new little furball.

"I know, I know," Alex says, reaching his arm to sweep me in front of him. He wraps me up in his hold and we both watch while Shelly joins Emily on the floor to get to know our new family member.

"I should have discussed this with you first, but I always wanted a puppy, and Father never allowed it. A lady was selling them out of the back of her truck. She had three left, and he started giving kisses right away. Seemed like he just fit, ya know? We'll get him checked at the vet, but she swore they'd all had their first shots— and—" He steps closer, and I feel his lips nuzzle against the side of my head. I smile at every bit of it. "And...I thought a father-daughter gift was in order for today."

"He's—it's—so perfect." I turn in his arms, snuggling in for a fast kiss.

"What is he?" Shelly stands and lifts the squirming dog into her arms, cradling him against her chest.

"He's a—mutt—doodle—poodle."

Shelly and I both laugh.

"Sounds manly," Shelly adds.

"Yeah, I know. Let's hope he doesn't grow up to be too big," Alex says, stepping away from me and bending forward to nuzzle his own nose against the pup's. "So what do you think, Em? What are we going to name him?"

Emily puts her finger to her mouth and rolls her eyes up, exaggerating her thinking as she rocks from side to side. It takes her exactly ten seconds to blurt out the name I knew was coming.

"Ajax! Like all the others!" She rushes to Shelly and insists on taking *Ajax* into her own arms.

"Alright then," Alex says, quirking a brow toward me. "Ajax it is. What do you say we go get his bed and crate and food out of the car?"

"Okay," Emily says, barely giving Alex attention. She's so in love with her new puppy, I'm not sure any of the rest of us will ever exist again.

"Just like all the others?" Alex whispers in my ear as he reaches to help Emily give the puppy back to Shelly.

I shrug.

"We've had a lot of random pets called Ajax. A caterpillar, a cricket, two fish and four rocks. She always calls them Ajax, because she couldn't say Alex when she was smaller. There hasn't been a single other name introduced by her for any pet in years."

Alex swallows at my explanation and spends a few extra seconds with both Emily and the puppy in his embrace. He's finally able to convince Emily and Shelly to help him with the puppy's things while I "babysit" the dog. Knowing Alex, he's probably bought out the entire pet store for this little guy.

"Mommy, we need to ask you a very important question," Emily announces as she traipses back into the house. She looks up and back over her shoulder, and I hear her whisper to Alex, "Did I do it right?"

"Just right," he says with a wink. "But remember, we need to get your mom outside onto the deck." Alex points his chin at the puppy. "Would you mind taking yourself and that little dog outside while we set something up?"

"Okay? Sure...?" That anxious patter is back in my chest, and I wonder how many puppies I can potty train at once. "Did you buy all three puppies? Is that what this is?"

I scoop up little Ajax hoping to God that's not what Alex is about to reveal. I won't be able to say *no*, but three puppies? That's a lot.

"No." Alex chuckles taking my hand in his and passes the puppy to Shelly as he walks me out to the rock. Emily catches up and holds my other hand, and before Alex can surprise me, our daughter gives it away, getting on her knee and holding an open jewelry box in her palm.

I gasp, and the tears hit my eyes hard and fast. "Mommy. Look."

"Alex!" I burst out his name, and he falls to one knee, taking the ring from Emily as she climbs to sit on his bent leg.

"Will you marry me," Alex says, adding, "will you marry *us?*"

Four words. Nothing more. Four utterly perfect words.

Us. He said *us*.

Throat closing, heart rushing into my head, all I can do is nod. Emily leaps up to clap and jump, tugging my hand closer to her daddy and pushing us together awkwardly.

We all start to laugh, and Shelly shouts "kiss, kiss, kiss" until Alex stretches his arm around my back and tilts me until my face is to the sky.

"More than the sun," he says against my mouth before taking my lips with his in a kiss that is as raw and desperate as it is sure and steady.

I continue nodding, and glance at my aunt Shelly, who's got tears streaming down her smiling face as Alex brings me back up to stand tall.

"Oh...wow... Alex...I..."

My answer is drowned with happy tears as he pushes the ring that was in the box onto my finger. It's a perfect, obviously antique ring. Perfect for me. It's platinum. One that has this nice patina to it. And there's these tiny accent diamonds that wrap around what must be at least two carrots in the center.

"I just need the one *yes* from you," Alex says through the softest, happiest and most hopeful smile I've ever seen. "What do you say?"

All I have ever wanted has just exploded into the real,

and I can't believe this is happening, that everything is working out—that he, and I, and the family I've waited so long to claim, might just be okay.

All of us. Together.

"Yes, Alex. Yes, Emily," I choke out, unable to push back the wave of my own shaking, trembling surge of pure happiness that has become me and my voice. I scoop up Emily, who's locked onto the squirming puppy. Alex's arms wrap around all of us. Everyone's smiling as I start bawling and laughing at the same time while the new puppy starts licking everyone's faces. "I will marry you. Yes!"

11.

ALEX, PRESENT DAY.

"Grady. Please. We're *brothers*." I stress the word how Father used to, grappling for shit that moves Grady, so I add, "We also have Father's legacy to go through, and again, I'm sorry. I've said it over and over. I'm sorry. Please call me back. I want to bury the hatchet. Dude...I'm willing to pay. To make it right by you. *I want* to make it up to you. Please let me; I'll do whatever it takes."

I sigh out loud and long so he can hear my frustration on the message, and so I can make it sound like he's won—because that's what my brother needs to feel.

I've left message after message for Grady. Groveled and groveled, begged and begged. He must be loving this shit. And I'm sure he thinks he's *owed* this kind of ass-kissing from me, but damn, his lack of response is concerning. It also makes me worry I've pushed him too far. Worse, when we're finally face-to-face, his lack of response combined with what he did to Jojo has pushed *me* too far. I'm afraid I won't be able to keep up the charade or hold myself back.

It will nearly kill me to not pound him into the dirt all over again. The guy beat up and tried to rape the girl I've loved for my entire life.

But—*fine*. I'll keep it together. I'll do anything it takes. I'll fake it and lie and lick his damn feet. Kiss his ass if needed. Because I'm going to marry Jojo tomorrow, and nothing else matters. My future is set in stone with love, with joy, and with more beauty and happiness than I could have ever imagined. All of that makes me more determined than ever to crack into my brother's black soul and find his heart and fill it up however he needs, to make Jojo and Emily safe.

My plan is to make peace, and if not peace—because let's be real, Grady and I have never once had that feeling between us—then I will nail his ass to the wall how my father taught me to do. I'll lock him in with signed contracts and hand over enough of the inheritance and the control of the company to satisfy him, but keep enough hooks and stipulations inside my deals that state he'll lose it all if he comes near my family ever again. One misstep, and he'll lose it all—to me.

As I exit the private, key-entry-only elevator that takes me from the parking garage all the way to my penthouse, I head for my walk-in closet and grab my newest, hand-tailored tuxedo. I pull out a pressed tux shirt, grab some gold cufflinks, as well as every tux tie, vest and cummerbund set I own, and shove them in a duffel bag.

I grimace as I realize that I own a lot of them; the bag is stuffed full. But silently, for once, I thank my mother's insistence. She set appointments with tailors for me regularly so that each year I could have a new set of tuxes, as well as a whole bunch of these ridiculous peacock accessories. I needed to be ready for all Sinclair events, including holiday parties and torturous dinners. I've worn this junk to a lot of them, but now Jojo will get to pick which ones she wants me to wear to our wedding.

A wedding that she's planning. Tomorrow at the lake.

Jojo and I.

Jojo, and I, and our Emily.

My heart swells with anticipation and pride as well as utter disbelief that I could be this lucky, and then it starts thumping again with worry and fears. As my mother's face and then Grady's face flashes in my mind, I swallow the boulder that's suddenly lodged in there. I wonder if maybe I'll never get to tell Jojo how the lake is both hers and mine and has been for years.

Maybe it doesn't even matter at this point?

If Grady resists, I'll have to sign the lake and my lake house over to him. He won't be able to resist it. It's a trump card he'll have to have.

Jojo and I worried over this point long into the early morning hours last night. She thinks letting go of the lake would be selling out my own heart. Hell, she's right!

Grady and my Father always planned to drain it and sell the water, then extract the oil out from underneath. She and I both know giving all of those rights away to Grady would be selling out Tacoma, too. It would be selling out my entire planet and everything I stand for.

But...fuck! Do I have any other choice? Not if we want to be a family, for Emily to be safe. She and I went over scenario after scenario, and we both decided that I will play my cards—the lake house and the aquifer—very close to my chest. For now, I'll wait. Showing Grady that I care about anything other than Jojo would be like showing my brother a second Achilles heel when I already have a huge one exposed.

Jojo.

Grady knows she's my weak point. I also need to save my strength and my protective focus for when my mother and Grady find out about Emily, because if we're talking about weak points here, Emily's appearance has ripped off my chest plate. I'll burn down the world and all that comes with it to keep her safe.

I know Emily's sudden presence could send my mother and Grady over the edge. Maybe not my mother, but Grady could take Emily personally. He could see her as some sort of inheritance threat, or worse, he could carry Father's torch on the hatred, and the feud, and the years of wanting to crush any and all Wallaces, and he will lose his mind.

Packing up my tux into a traveling bag, I silently thank God yet again that my father's dead and buried in the ground. I wish he were buried deeper. Under cement.

Emily's appearance would have changed Father's game. He would have considered her a monster. He told me over and over again while I was in high school that he would never permit a bastard born of me and a Wallace. It's why I never slept with Jojo, not until that last night. It was one of Father's many rules and commands: *Do what you want with her but never, ever, risk knocking her up.* His words, not mine.

It was one of the commands I'd meant to keep, too, simply because Jojo's first time should have been with anyone other than her lying, Sinclair, fucked-up, fake boyfriend. Who murdered her father. Add that detail in and just...hell no! I swore to myself I'd never touch her like that. But when she asked me—begged me—took off her clothes and asked me again, I was weak. I let it happen because I wanted to be that guy with her just once, the kind she deserved, before I told her the truth.

We have Emily to show for it, a creature of perfection, of her mother's heart and soul, and nothing terrible from me. I can't imagine Emily not being on this earth. She is the best rule of my father's that I ever broke.

Shaking off my thoughts, I drag everything I need for the wedding into the living room so I can spread it out and check off the list Shelly gave to me. After I get the tux, my next job is to land some flowers to bring back with me, and then I'll be done.

My feet echo loudly on the marble, and as I drop the

stuff on the leather couch, I look around, thinking that I won't miss this place when I sign it over to Grady. It's cold and stark and filled with everything that has made me sad. He can have it.

Realizing I need the fancy black socks that go with my outfit and the dumb, shiny shoes to complete it as well, I turn back, but as I head down the window-walled hallway, my eyes shift to the Tacoma city street below. I'm drawn to the sight like a magnet to metal. My mother's Mercedes is below. No question, that is her car and that is my mother!

She's staring up at my penthouse, stiff and unmoving, like a ghost or a zombie. Her face is drawn and pale, and she's incredibly tense. I can tell by the rise in her shoulders and the stillness she stands with. Stiffer than normal. Maybe it's the light, or the distance, but she looks positively unwell.

I grab my phone and command, "Call Mother."

My mother picks up before the first ring is completed.

She was waiting for me to spot her. What the *fuck?*

"What are you doing?" I ask my mother. "I see you out there, and you don't look good. Are you...sick? Are you just trying to come up?" I soften my tone. "Please, can you? Come up? I'll buzz you in and fix you something."

As much as I distrust her, I have also never seen her look like this.

"I can't," she says, voice tight. Still keeping my call

connected, she quickly leaps back into her car as though she doesn't want anyone to see her. She's hiding from something. Grady?

Ever since the funeral, she's been acting odd—looking odd—and behaving kind of crazy. I've left it alone, figuring it's probably grief. I thought maybe my mother didn't know how to function without my father beating her and telling her what to do. Now that Shelly and Jojo have told me that she's been following Jojo around town and stalking the antique shop, I feel like I need to get to the bottom of her motives.

"Mother," I say gently. "What are you doing? Why won't you come up?"

"I...I'm not supposed to be here. It's off schedule."

"What do you mean? It's your life. You can be anywhere you want." I glance at the time; it's around two, which is when my mom usually works out at her club. Maybe that's what she means.

Changing the subject, I ask, "Have you heard from Grady?"

"Yes. What you did to him, Alex...he was hurt, and now he's very upset. He thinks you tried to kill him."

I did. I keep that blunt honesty to myself, though.

"He and I were just...overwrought. The funeral, you know." I flush, feeling guilty, but more angry imagining how Grady probably cried like a little baby to Mother about how I'm a terrible person. I'm sure he never once mentioned to her that he tried to rape Jojo.

I take the higher ground and don't bring it up. "I'm

trying to apologize to him. I'm aware it got out of hand, and I want to make amends."

Her breathing is heavy, like she's stressed, or like she's been running. I wonder again if she's ill. "Mother—hey, are you okay?" I show my concern, something we rarely did while Father was alive, but by how she's acting, my gut says I need to genuinely worry.

"Haven't been feeling myself, actually," she whispers.

"Is Grady trying to tell you what to do? Is he bossing you around? Because if he's doing that, it's not okay, and I hope you'll tell me," I probe, assuming that Grady's taken over the roll my Father left behind.

I soften my voice, feeling bad that I've been having this honeymoon-island-type experience with Jojo, and I haven't even reached out to my mom since the funeral. Despite how twisted our family is, I should have.

"Mother. Please let me know if there's something I can do for you."

"There isn't. Unless…the topic of Jojo—"

"I know. I know. That's why I've been practically MIA," I explain. "I suppose you can tell that we've reconnected. We're still in love, Mother. I'm going to marry her. I'd like your blessing on that if it's at all possible."

I hear her pull in a sharp breath.

"Can't you *please* come up and we'll talk about it? This is so important to me, Mom. And I want you here for it."

"No! Oh, God…no! Do not marry her!" she shrieks, sounding near insane and sort of like how Father used to shriek at us. *"You cannot marry that girl. You can't do that!* I will *not* give my blessing for such a...disaster! Don't you see, Alex? If you do that, you will risk everything. It's too dangerous, Alex. *No.*"

"It's happening." I'm matter-of-fact. My disappointment in her reaction has swallowed up my previous expectations. I didn't truly think this conversation would go well when I had it. "It's happening tomorrow, Mother. Maybe tonight, and I thought about inviting you, but considering your reaction, I suppose you can just send me a card."

"No!" She shrieks again. "You don't understand."

I run a hand through my hair and press my forehead against the cool glass wishing I had the inner strength to hang up on her right now. I stare at the top of her unmoving car. Her voice cracks then breaks and, shit—I think the woman is crying.

"Alex...I came here, hoping that you'd see me. I'm not supposed to tell you, but you probably know. You need to get that Wallace girl—*get everyone*—out of here. It's not safe, and if you marry her here, I'm afraid, Alex. For me, for her—for *anyone* that Jojo loves. Get. Them. Out! Go now. Forget about this silly wedding business. Please. There is too much at stake, Alex. You know what I'm talking about...*too much at stake.*"

My thoughts spin wildly with paranoia. *Does my mother know about Emily? Is that what she's talking about? Has someone seen the little girl running around the lake house? Are they fucking spying on us, or is Mother simply talking about the 'family business' being at stake? Fuck!*

My voice grows shaky even though I don't want it to, but I strive hard to keep it calm, to remember the joy and the love waiting for me, and I work to keep my past and my personal paranoias shut down. Just in case, I ask, "Are *you* personally threatening Jojo, Mother? Are *you* the one putting her at risk? Is that what you mean, because I don't think you mean it. Answer me if that's the case."

I probe her hard, trying to get her to bring up a sighting of a little girl or child. I need to see if she will slip up and say too much. "I know you've been stalking them both. Following them. Me. Tell me why? Why would you want to hurt Jojo now, Mother. There's no point in it. The feud was Father's not yours. Please tell me you're not carrying it on for him. Please."

"No. Not me. I've haven't been trying to hurt Jojo— I've been watching and trying to get her to go, and waiting. This is all too much for me, though. I'm afraid. It's just not safe. Never been safe." She trails off, her voice starting to shake as much as mine, and then something I've never heard before happens.

My mother isn't just crying. She's sobbing. "Not safe."

"She will be safe with me, Mother. Safe as my wife."

"No." Mother cries more.

The pity I've hidden from her surges forward. My mother married a monster. She had two children with this monster, and my father broke her. Probably by hurting Grady and I when we were babies, a tactic I'm certain he used to keep her in line. I can imagine Father setting my Mother up just how he set me up—year after year pretending one thing and then *bam*...pulling the rug out from under her. He must have let my mother watch Grady and I crash and burn the same way I was forced to let Jojo rise and fall. Maybe she was told to zoom in and scoop up the pieces. Or worse, maybe she wasn't even allowed that luxury.

From the way she's acting, maybe she's finally shedding some of what she went through. I know she must have lived what we lived—how we lived—always in fear, always in a state of torture, but she needs to be able to talk about it on her own time.

"Mother," I call out to her, trying again just in case she needs to finally vent. "Come up. I've got tea...I can make you some...soup?"

"I can't do it anymore, Alex. I can't," She sobs harder.

"Please...Mother. You don't have to do anything you don't want to do, not anymore. Father's gone and he can't hurt you or me or Grady anymore," I say gently.

For some reason her grief is finding all of these holes in my heart that I'd punched out every time she didn't show up to defend me, and her tears are filling the holes back up with things I swore I didn't have for her. Concern. Worry. Empathy. Maybe more. Maybe...love?

"Just listen to me, please. You don't have to answer, but try to listen." Over her wracking sobs, I pull in a huge breath and boldly go on. "I—hell, Mother. *We've* been through so much. And no one who knew Father will ever blame you if you were the one who pulled the trigger on him, especially not me. If that's what you're worried about, I want you to know I'll never judge you. If you killed him, the world would consider you in the right...maybe you *were* right to do it."

She gasps loudly as if my words shock her, but her crying lessens like she's trying to hear me better. My heart sinks at the idea that I'm correct in my assumptions, then it slightly soars to think that my suspicions *must* be true. Her complete lack of denial here makes me almost certain my mother *did* kill my father. And she'd done it as some sort of rebellion, finally.

"And if it *was* you," I forge on, "I suppose I can only thank you for it, because you've had the courage none of us could find. You've also given me a chance at a future I never even hoped to imagine. In a few short days, because Jojo came back, I've found my life again. I've recovered my happiness, and I just got my whole entire soul back after Father stole it away and sold it underground. I thought I didn't have a chance at any of those things, and maybe, if you can get Grady to call me, I can give him some sort of happiness back, too. I know Grady and I are different, but maybe if I can give him what he *thinks* he deserves, all of the money and power of our name, maybe all of us can be a little happy now. We deserve it, Mother. We all do."

"Ever the optimistic one," she whispers. "You've

suffered for that, because you're like me, my poor, dreamy young son."

"It's not a dream anymore. Don't you see? Anything's possible."

Her breathing grows more ragged, and I hear a fresh round of sniffles and movement. She's probably rustling for one of her linen handkerchiefs.

I want to tell her about Emily, tell her that she's got a granddaughter and confirm what I suspect she maybe knows—that Jojo had her own secrets—but I hold that part back, just in case.

It's too new, not safe, and my mother's obviously unstable right now. Hell, she may even be a murderer. I want her to know that in my eyes I see her as savior also. She was so psychologically abused. We all were. No court of law would ever find her guilty, but I can tell by the sound of her broken voice that she feels it as deeply as I do. Maybe she's felt it all along.

Whatever happens, and even if I never see her again, which is likely once we leave this place, I want her to remember this conversation. She deserves to know that my heart is with hers, that I'm still like her, wherever she and I end up on this earth.

"Your tears break my heart, Mother. I know Father wouldn't let you ever comfort us because it kept us 'soft.'" I say that last word using Father's scornful tone. "But I want you to know that I understand how much and how deeply you've been hurt, too. And I...thank you for..."

"Please don't thank me for anything, son. It is completely undeserved."

"You're wrong. Let me finish." I swallow down the stones blocking my throat, and push back my own tears at her words, because the part of me that has always blamed her suddenly understands all too well how she got trapped. Now that I have a child of my own, I suddenly understand it's possible my mother had been Father's most extreme victim.

"I thank you for my very life. And know that I know that I'm going to be okay. I will live the rest of my life, the one you gave me, very well. I'm going to take Jojo—and Aunt Shelly and Walt and." I pause as I almost say Emily's name. "And I'll go away with them. I will go with everyone that Jojo loves and get them away from here. I won't come back, but one day, Mother, I hope you will be able to come visit me."

I pull in a shaking breath.

"I also really want you to believe that we're going to be happy. Very happy, and *God*, Mother...I pray, and I wish, for you to be happy now too. You can, you know? You can."

She laughs out. This small self-deprecating laugh as though she thinks I'm a fool, but in case I can break through to her, I press on. "We still have whole lives we can live. Even you. What's left of us can be good. I want that for the three of us—you, me and Grady. We can be like..." I search my mind for the right words, for something that will resonate with her. "Like...those big Aspen trees that have bends at their bases because of the giant blizzards they survived in the past. Trees that, up top, *do* eventually grow thick, and strong, and straight because their branches have always reached for the sun. It's the tops and it's the reaching for light that matters. Those trees, they create bright green leaves every summer. They make a jaw-dropping color show every fall, and they never look down to their bases. Only up to the sky. Do you understand me, Mother? Do you think you can just look up to the sky from now on?"

"Yes, Alex. But I'm so afraid," she whispers softly. The crying seems to have stopped, and she's composed herself. After a long pause, and three deep breaths, she says so quietly I can hardly hear. "I'll tell Grady to stop pouting. He'll call you soon. I'll make sure it happens as long as you promise me you will take Jojo away."

"I promise, Mother," I say, pulling air back into my lungs. "Thank you," I say once more before she ends our call.

It's not what I wished deep in my heart to say to her, and of course it's not what I wished to hear back, either. I wish, like I've always wished with my family for my entire life, that I could just be a normal son with normal parents. I want to be a man who can tell his mother that he loves her the day before he gets married. One who could hear it back—and believe it. My heart is at least satisfied she listened to my whole speech about being happy without hanging up.

I think maybe she understands. Maybe she will go

toward the light. If she can only see that she didn't murder our father—her husband.

She saved her two sons.

I think of Emily's smile. Jojo's sparkling eyes. My future with them.

My mother...she saved everything.

12.

JOJO, PRESENT DAY.

Seeing the bride before the ceremony is welcoming bad luck Alex and I can't afford. I believe in us, and I know he feels the same. It's those damn outside forces, though, that make superstitions hold their weight.

I swore I would be good and stay here, on the other side of the house, away from Alex until Shelly led me to the ceremony—until she and Emily appear to tell me it's time...tomorrow. I made no guarantees about what I would do the night before the wedding, though.

Lingerie has always been a fantasy for me. I've never had a reason to wear it, and when Alex and I were young, I didn't have the means to buy it, nor did I know where to go shopping for it.

While Alex was off getting his tux and trying to reconcile with Grady, I made a special, sneaky, and very careful trip to town where, with sunglasses on and only twenty minutes to shop, I couldn't decide between two things. One was a very sexy, white lace bra and panty set —reserved for the wedding tomorrow—and the other was this amazing, slightly wild corset thing that has a panty with...well...access.

I was so amped up to wear it for Alex, but he was holed up in his office drawing up papers with his attorneys over the phone. Apparently, handing over an entire business to one's brother takes a whole bunch of time, number crunching and typing.

I made it through the dinner without Alex, and then made it through Emily and Shelly's pre bedtime chatter. I had to gush once more over the gorgeous tulle and flower-embroidered dresses Alex had brought back with him for Emily for the wedding tomorrow.

In Shelly's room, she and I whispered and giggled over how my aunt managed to find a website where she's now legal to officiate the wedding tomorrow. When I left, I told her to listen for any sounds of Emily trying to wake up and to please intercept her so Alex and I could be alone—very alone—which is when I blushed bright red and told her about the corset I'd bought. She laughed so hard she cried when I told her about the lessons the store manager had to give me in order to get both in and out of the thing. She assured me that in the end, it wouldn't matter.

I gave Emily final kisses and have waited a good forty minutes on the other side of the house just to be sure Emily was asleep. And then I waited at least twenty more before texting Alex.

You coming out of there? I miss you.

Miss you a lot.

I started to amp it up when more time passed.

Want to go to bed? With...me?

Last night as a 'bachelor!'

I eventually put the corset on and took a picture of the cherry-red lace stretched taut across my breasts, making sure the small slits in the center where the peaks of my breasts pushed through was very clear in the photograph.

I sent it along without any words at all. I resulted to porn, basically.

It wasn't long before the knocking started.

I barely got the door open before Alex's mouth covered mine and his hands cupped the sides of my face. He walked me backward and closed the door behind him, pausing our steps to lock it with the flick of his hand.

I backed my way up to the giant king-sized bed and stood still, chewing my lip nervously so he could take in all of me—corset and matching panties.

This thing pushed my breasts up extra high, and I saw his eyes flick to the part where the corset met the panties. His gaze trailed to where the lace was thin, and wide open in the bottom. I spread my legs just enough and he audibly growled.

With deliberate steps, he caught up to me and lifted me under my arms, setting me on the bed and spreading my knees forcefully as he slid his palms down my front, feeling the skin of my breasts pushing through the corset, then tugging hard on my nipples that had hardened into tight nubs through the slits.

"Goddamn, you're beautiful," he said, looking down at me with searing eyes and gritted teeth.

For once, more than beautiful...I felt sexy.

He caged me in his arms, lowered his head and bit my nipple hard as I arched up into him, wanting him to taste more of me. His hands slid under my back and he pushed me into his mouth as he sucked until my tips were raw and I was moaning and melting.

His scratchy stubbled chin drew down the center of the lace along my chest until he reached the bow at my belly button where he tugged at it with his teeth to untie it as well as pepper my belly with soft kisses.

His gentle touch gave way to his rougher side quickly, though, his hands rushing up the center of my thighs until they found the place where the fabric split. Alex's thumbs pulled the seams apart as his tongue took long, torturous sweeps over my clit. I came quickly, and so hard that my legs wrapped around his neck in an attempt to keep his mouth right where it was.

That was only the beginning, though, and Alex stood quickly, tugging his pants and his boxers, getting them down just enough to pull his cock out and into his hand. In a swift movement, he shoved through the slit fabric to push himself inside me, thrusting so hard that I eventually was moved all the way to the top of the bed frame. Alex ground into me, his breath heavy and his eyes colored by lust, until the fabric of my panties finally tore and exposed all of me just in time for him to come hard.

He pulled out, his fingers still prowling over my body, taking bites, licks and tastes while stealing more touches from every bit of my heated, sweat-shimmering body for minutes until he made me come a second time. Finally, he tore himself away and slipped back into his office leaving me to sleep.

Lying there, I read his texts while my hand glided over the raw spots on my breasts he'd made, relishing in the pain mixed with pleasure that lingers.

You will stay in that room for the rest of the night and not come out until Shelly gets you. I'll send in Emily tomorrow, and I'll send in food and Shelly says she's got a dress for you. Just in case that doesn't work, I've also got some back-ups so you'll have no excuses not to marry me. All I want to do is come back in there and make love to you all night long, which is why I'll be hiding and taking cold showers in the guest room.

I bite at my lip and laugh as my body rushes with the memories of his touch. I can't wait to show him what I bought for our wedding night. He's going to go insane.

I'm startled into laughing more when his next message comes in.

And you will buy a new pair of panties just like those I ruined so we can do that again.

And then...

In fact, buy two.

Now that it's morning, I slip into the white bridal set, pushing my breasts up high in the crystal-studded bra cups. The wispy, lace panties hang on my hips, and I sit on the edge of the bed to slide the silk stalkings up my legs and hook the tops to the garter belt.

Last night was my dark angel coming out, and today he gets the good one.

Good until I decide to be naughty, I muse to myself, smiling at the memories of last night.

My aunt knocks lightly at my door, and I hide behind it as I open it slowly, calling out "I'm not quite—decent" to make sure it's not Emily awake too early or Alex trying to get a peek at the bride ahead of time.

"I've got your grandmother's dress," she says, shoving her way inside with a large box. "If it doesn't fit, Alex had the bridal shop send over a couple of other choices, but let's start with this one."

"Okay," I say, working hard to steel myself for possible disappointment. My mother's dress was lost in the fire, but Shelly, she's had a way of hanging onto things her entire life. It's why she's in the antique business.

"This box hasn't been touched in over sixty years. Let's hope the moths haven't gotten inside." She grins excitedly as she takes a half-damp cloth to wipe the layer of dust away from the box's lid. I cough as she opens it, worried that the dress buried inside will be too yellow to wear today.

She peels back layers of cotton and aged paper before finally unfurling heavy folds of satin over the bed. My grandmother's dress is stunning, an old fashioned, princess cut ballgown.

"It's so perfect," I say, running my hand along the beadwork that my own grandmother did herself as a young girl. Too young to marry, but married all the same. It isn't my mom's, but it's just as special.

"I knew you'd love it," Shelly says, working up the skirt with her hands and lifting the dress so I can slide up and underneath. "Walt had to help me get it down from the rafters. Now, let's see how I can make this thing fit."

I pause, realizing my uncle Walt is here, too. He's the closest thing to a dad that I have. It's hunting season, and for him, that's everything.

"He came home...for this?" I meet Aunt Shelly's eyes, mine becoming glossy.

"Oh honey, of course he did. I'm not promising more than the ceremony, though. You know that man and those damn ducks. It's half the reason we're still together—I can count on him being gone for long stretches at a time." We both laugh at Walt's expense, but I know every word she spoke was with love. She loves her independence, and she loves how Walt's obsessions and quirks fit into the mix. What would she stuff and mount, after all, if he didn't like to prowl around the woods for weeks on end?

I've been told that I look a lot like my grandmother. It's something both of my parents said, and I hope it means our figures weren't very different. I swim up the lining and my body makes its way through the skirt and into the tight bodice. I suck in my stomach and feel for the arm holes.

"There are so many buttons!" I marvel at the long line of pearl-sized buttons and the little eye hooks that are supposed to go over each one to close the dress.

"Ahh, yes. Zippers were only for the *cheap* gowns back then." My aunt's deft fingers get to work, and as it closes along my back, I wriggle my way all the way in. After she closes the last button, she begins smoothing out the layers, pulling and tugging at the skirt that drapes over my hips and down my legs, falling in classic sweeps befitting of a dress worn during the second World War.

"Oh, honey. It fits like a glove."

Her voice is smothered in emotion, and I prepare myself to turn and take my image in from the mirror behind me.

Twisting my neck, I look over the back first, loving the effect of the buttons linked all the way up my spine and how they make my waist seem so narrow. They end just between my shoulder blades where the dress is open, exposing the skin of my upper back. The soft sleeves fall off my shoulders just right, and the princess cut hugs my waist, folds of fabric reflecting the light and casting sweeps of shadows over my hips until the dress stops at my ankles.

"Just one last thing," my aunt says, reaching deep into her pocket and pulling out a Cameo broach that I recognize.

"This was my mom's!" I choke out.

Shelly nods. "You're mother had lent it to me—I'd forgotten I had it until long after you moved away. I've been saving it for you."

We both try to get our emotions back in order as Shelly takes the broach and tugs at the gathering in the center of my chest enough to keep me from getting stuck with the sharp end as she pushes the pin through and clasps it straight in the center.

"There. Something old. I guess *two* things old." She smiles, satisfied.

I lean forward and take her hands with mine and our foreheads fall into one another lightly. "I love you, Aunt Shelly."

"I love you too." She sighs. "You're so beautiful. Your mom, and your grandmother...they would have loved to see this."

"I feel like they're here, like they *can* see me. I know they can feel my happiness all the way up to heaven."

"Of this, I'm sure." Shelly grins, walking backward with me so we can look at the dress all over again in the full-length mirror.

My hair is tucked up with hidden bobby pins and the length curls loosely down my back.

"Mommy!" Emily barrels into the room, all zipped up into the little white dress we'd all agreed she'd wear for the ceremony. "I've brought your shoes! They were in the kitchen and Daddy thinks you'll need them. He's all ready to go. He looks so funny and nervous, and I'm not supposed to tell you any of the surprises but there are so many of those out there, and you should see what Ajax has to wear and..." She comes to an instant stop, grinning ear-to-ear just before she says breathlessly, "You look like a real princess!"

"So do you, honey." I bend slowly and hug her, afraid to tear the old dress.

Emily sets down the simple pair of silk slippers. "Good work, Emily." Shelly smiles. "Those came with the dress."

I'm instantly grateful that they aren't heels. They look almost like ballet shoes, only the top is marked with a thin row of pearls.

"They're probably real." My aunt runs a finger over the line of round, iridescent balls.

"That's intimidating, considering I'm bound to trip over my feet and pop them off." I joke, only it's not really a joke. I'm not really steady on my feet—especially now that I'm dizzy with happiness.

I put each shoe on carefully, one at a time, and Aunt Shelly holds up a thin wire band wrapped in twists of wildflowers and leaves, something she made herself last night by collecting anything and everything beautiful that grows around the lake.

Smiling, and with Emily looking on with eyes big and bright, I bend forward so Shelly can pin it to my head.

"What about a veil, Mommy?"

"I wanted to make sure I saw everything clearly today, with my own eyes and my own heart. A veil might get in the way of that."

My answer makes my daughter smile and nod once in agreement. Shelly pins a miniature flower-and-leaf band on to Emily's head next, then she asks both of us, "Are you two ready?"

I slide my hand into Emily's, and together we both face our last living relative. I search deep in her eyes to make sure she's clear of reservations. I see nothing but joy.

"Yes. I'm ready."

"Me, too," my daughter pipes in, adding in a very loud shout for one so small, *"Daddy here we come!"*

13.

ALEX, PRESENT DAY.

I'm nearly brought to my knees as Jojo and Emily walk towards me wearing white dresses, smiling.

Jo's dress couldn't be more perfect, and I can tell, even from a distance, that it's special—*old*. Emily is perfection, too, the skirt of her dress swaying along the space between her ankles and knee as she exaggerates her steps, her face scrunched up and serious for such a formal occasion. She's trying to act so grown up, and all I want to do is run up to her, lift her to the sky, and beg her to stay young and innocent like this forever.

This moment, it's surreal, a dream, and it's all I've ever imagined. I can't believe they're on their way "to marry me." Just last night, before she hugged me to say goodnight, Emily linked our pinky fingers and said she was promising to be connected to me forever, and today it's really happening.

I'm in a trance as Jojo steps closer and walks across

our rock with her confident gait. The beaded lace that swirls around the entire dress wraps around her waist, making her look like she's stepped out of another time. The heavy folds of fabric that look as though they're made for a queen to wear drape off of her narrow hips. The dresses Aunt Shelly had me purchase last minute as backups don't even come close to it in scope and beauty. I'm caught on the way her hand—the left one—engagement ring winking at me in the sunlight, gathers up the front of the gown as her feet find their balance so she can move along the rock. When she reaches my side, she lets go and the dress falls in a heavy cascade, swinging around us both with its grandeur.

And just like the first time we met, during that summer before our freshman year, Jojo turns her twinkling eyes up and locks them onto mine. She has this look about her. She's glowing, and I'm filled with this sensation that she's someone from another world.

A magical being. A girl...*out for a little adventure.*

The thought activates a grin, and though I try to fight it, I feel one side of my lips twisting up. Jojo notices, tilting her head ever so slightly, her own smile starting to form. My heart jolts and then settles into pure joy.

Her long, waving brown hair is down and has become a part of the wind and the lake, exactly how I love it. It's wild, like the storms that brew over the ocean and rush onto land. Wild...like her. Her face is void of any makeup, except what appears to be the littlest bits of mascara and an almost imperceptible shade of gray beneath her eyes. The red in her cheeks I recognize as her own brand of Jojo's heated blushing.

Little Emily, the person that I still can't get over how she's somehow half Jojo, half me, and completely herself, is clinging fiercely to her mother's hand. Ajax, not to be outdone, is trailing behind our daughter, a fat tulle bow around his neck, his full belly nearly dragging under him as he gets one puppy tooth hooked into Emily's dress. As though Emily's been coached on what to do, she walks her mother all the way to Walt first, dragging Ajax along with her the entire way. Walt takes Jojo's arm and Emily picks up her hand. Then, they all come to me, and she and Walt both place Jojo's hand into mine. Emily's little face goes even more stoic as she folds our hands together, slipping hers in between ours. Walt, grinning, clasps his hand on top of them all, ceremoniously bonding the three of us together.

When that's completed, Emily breaks out into giggles as Ajax nearly pulls her backwards into the lake in his puppy vs. fluffy-white-dress, tug-of-war game.

Shelly, Jojo and I grab Emily but can't resist laughing, too, as we help the puppy and Emily get untangled. The three of us, this time minus the puppy making trouble, line up again. The puppy is finally flopped down for a nap. We have no other audience, so however and wherever we end up is the perfect place to be as long as we're together.

Shelly looks the part of a perfect officiator in a

formal black dress. It's probably from the antique shop where she dug up Jojo's dress. She's also managed to find a rather nice white cape that adds a formal yet whimsical drama to what she's about to do for us. I nod to her then turn my attention back to my bride, leaning in close enough to whisper. "You look stunning. I'm the happiest man on earth right now, Jojo."

"Thank you," she says, her lips wrapping around the words slowly. Her eyes blink closed as she looks down and touches the length of her gown. "It was my grand-mother's."

I nod in appreciation as she adds, "And you also look —hot." Her blush fires into her cheeks. "And…so you know, I'm the happiest *woman* on earth right now."

"Thanks for marrying me, Jojo." She flushes more and nods, biting her lip and keeping silent, this time because I can see she's choked up.

I know how much marriage, and standing up with me in a white dress passed down through the Wallace family, must mean to her. She's always been about family and symbols. And because I've always been all about making her happy, knowing that she's so moved right now has taken my heart all the way to the moon, brought up pricks of moisture at my own eyes, and has robbed me of my words too.

When Jojo and I clam up, Shelly helps us along by pulling a phone out of her pocket that's already turned on and is running FaceTime. "First things first. Jeff has to be part of this! You there, Jeff?"

"I'm here, lovebirds. And I couldn't be happier with what is happening here today."

Jojo and Emily laugh and shout out happily, "Jeff! Jeff!"

I smile at the grinning man in the phone. "Thank God. I needed a best man. I was feeling very out numbered."

Jeff laughs from the phone. "Happy to have the job, and welcome to the family."

I let that word sink inside me for just a beat. *Family*. That word has always been this illusive thing to me. Something that I craved, but that I thought would never really be for me. That it would only mean things like rules, cruelty, danger and revenge. If Jojo becomes a Sinclair today, Jojo and Emily, then the word *family* will mean what it should. Love. Unconditional, beautiful love. And I'm glad Jeff is a part of it—*us*.

"Thank you, Jeff." I nod and smile, making sure to pause and receive his genuine expression of happiness back.

After a few more seconds of nervous laughter, we prop Jeff on a deep divot in the rock, next to where I've placed every white orchid available for purchase from every flower shop in Tacoma. We want to be sure he's able to see the entire wedding area, as well as the morning view of the lake, right along with us.

He and Walt will serve as our witnesses, signing electronically as is the new tradition for hurried, modern weddings. We've brought the best of the old and new together for this, and even though I'm sad that my mother—no one from my family at all, actually—is here with me, I'm also relieved. It's too soon to introduce Emily, and though I hope my mother will come around and let go of some of the hurt we've all suffered, I'm not willing to risk Emily's happiness or safety to help bring about the changes she's facing in her own life. For my mom to come around, it will take time, and with her, it's possible I'm simply being my usual, overly optimistic self.

When I return to Jojo's side, Emily sits down next to Ajax on the rock, and JoJo and I both look at Shelly again, letting her show us how to proceed. Luckily, she did her homework, and quickly shushes Jeff and Emily who've been babbling to each other on and off this whole time.

"I'm a Lutheran," Shelly starts, drawing everyone silent. "And though this is not a Lutheran wedding, I find the vows said at the traditional ceremonies to be very romantic and appropriate for you two. So I've written them out on a card for each of you."

She pauses to pull two white cards out of her cape pocket and hands one to me and one to Jojo.

"There." She continues. "You're to read the vows out loud and add in your names where I drew the blank lines. Can you do that?"

We both nod, glancing at one another and smirking because Shelly is using that *teacher* voice, like we're school children.

"Jojo. Ladies first."

Jojo looks at the card and with zero hesitation begins with, "I, Jojo Wallace—uh—soon to be Jojo Sinclair?" She bites her lip, then breathes out nervously, glancing around our tiny group and back at me before saying, "I take you, Alex Sinclair, to be my husband, and these things I promise you: I will be faithful to you." She pauses to lock into my gaze before glancing down to quickly read more. "And...and I will be honest with you; I will respect, trust, help, and care for you."

She sighs and smiles, like she's reading ahead and likes what it says. "I will share my life with you, Alex. I will forgive you as we have been forgiven." The hand that she's had nestled in mine squeezes mine as hard as she can at those words.

I squeeze back, because knowing her, she's forgiving me all over again. I know without a doubt that with this hand squeeze here, and the way her eyes are boring into mine, that Jojo is asking me to please, finally, totally forgive myself.

When I smile at her, my eyes send out the message that I have—that I am forgiven—and that she's finally done that for me. She or God, because I must be forgiven if I'm getting to have the happy ending I never thought would belong to me.

She seems to understand, and nods once, turning her gaze back to the card. "And...I...will try with you to be better. To understand ourselves, the world, and God; through the best and worst of what is to come, and as long as we both shall live." Her voice has turned all raspy, and shaky, and sweet, and when she looks at me next, I again feel there's a higher power here with us. It's like God, or the universe, or all of the stars in the sky have finally aligned.

This beautiful redemption is erasing so much of the darkness and guilt that is still inside of me. It's lifting me up so high that I'm looking down on it all—on Jojo and Emily. My new family is real, and it's mine forever now, and I know, right in this moment, that I'm somehow getting a gift. I'm utterly *reborn.*

I cry openly as I say the beautiful vows she said to me, right back to her. Each and every line uttered to Jojo, in the creation of this new contract and union between us, heals me. It elevates me, and at the end I've been humbled completely by this new feeling of gratitude that's in my heart.

I turn to my daughter who's now lounging on her back, staring up at the sky, completely oblivious, taking for granted, just how she should, the fact that her parents have just transformed into *one* right in front of her. "Emily," I whisper, smiling down at her. "Remember? The rings? It's your turn."

"Oh. Yes." She hops up quickly, shakes out her dress and turns to both of us. She pulls the three rings I gave to her, all tied up into one big bow, out of her little pocket, then unties them, placing them together in the palm of her left hand. With a smile, she first slides my wedding band onto my finger and says, "I marry you to me." She turns her attention to her mother's solid platinum ring next, sliding that one on, saying, "I marry you to me, too, Mommy."

Jojo and I take the little ring we had made for her and place it together on her tiny left hand ring finger. "And we marry you too, Emily," Jojo adds.

Emily pulls in a deep breath and says formally, "Now we are all married. One family. Forever and ever." She shares a nod with me, which nearly cracks me up because I'm so proud that she remembered what I told her to say, but before I can congratulate her, she adds her own ending. "Married until the rest of our whole lives. And…then…" She sighs out, picking up both of our hands and presenting them as if we've both tied a wrestling match, "and then they all lived happily ever after. The end."

Her proud little grin is as bright as a comet, and it explodes into all of us.

Shelly crumples into tears, and even Jeff starts sobbing from the phone on the rock. Walt smiles somewhere underneath a scraggly beard, and Jojo and I—we do as she said.

We start to live right away…*happily.*

14.

JOJO, PRESENT DAY.

After the ceremony, we all had a nice dinner together. Making it more special, Jeff hung out with us on the phone the entire time. His approval, as well as how he truly believes he hasn't *abandoned* us by accepting a job far away, means everything to me.

Emily was the one who insisted on dancing and with everyone, and once I announced to her that it was her bedtime, she went with Walt and Shelly, while Alex told me he'd set up a surprise. He took me back out to the lake and then down to the little dock where he kissed me and directed me to put on a pair of Chucks. With a smile that melted my heart, he asked if I'd take a walk with him. I agreed quickly, and then he led me in a direction we never go—along what looked to be a freshly trodden pathway that went off from the backside of the deck, away from the lake.

I thought for a while that maybe he had another

place nearby that I never noticed—a guest home or something like his parents' boat house. Or like his father's old hunting lodge that's located at the other end of the lake. We've been walking for a while now, though, so whatever it is...it isn't an easy walk from the main house.

"It's not far," Alex says, as if he can read my mind. He keeps smiling that sexy-secretive smile of his, ducking us under branches and past bushes, until he leads me through this thicket of trees and out into a little meadow. It's a sparkling scene that can only be described as magical and made of dreams and wishes.

My dreams and wishes—ones I didn't even know I had.

Somehow, there is an oasis out here. With the use of some very large and long extension cords, Alex has strung lights through the branches all around us. Linen drapes in the shape of a tent with thick hemp ropes to hold the panels in place. All of it, placed above a king-sized mattress covered in down-feather and fleece blankets, and easily twenty pillows, and side tables with candles—all of it set up to make the perfect outdoor retreat for us to be alone.

I feel like I'm part of some magazine photoshoot, walking around the fairy forest he built for me. "When and how did you do this?" I whisper in awe, pausing to kiss his lips as we enter the structure.

"I have my ways." He's looking at me with heat in his eyes. "I just thought we'd need our own space away from the house, and Shelly and Walt, and Emily. Just for tonight."

"It's perfect." I nod, smiling while shaking my head at every detail around me. "Is it strange that I'm nervous?" I kick off my slippers and step onto the soft bedding and mattress before I look up at the glowing tent ceiling.

"Not at all, considering what went down between us last night," he says with an impish wink, following me inside.

"Panty ripper." I laugh.

His lip rises on the right, and his cheek dimples, the shadow of his stubble making it even darker and more pronounced.

"You're so beautiful." I stare, heart fluttering, wondering why I'm suddenly so timid.

He stares back. "*You* are. Always."

I run my hand along one of the linen walls and it waves at my touch.

"I can make a fire...if you want." He points to this awesome metal fire pit, already loaded up with kindling.

"That sounds nice, even though it's not cold, is it?" I move toward him.

Alex shakes his head and pulls his tux jacket off, laying it down to the side of the bed area. He uncuffs and rolls his sleeves up. The muscles of his forearms flex with the slight movement, reminding me how they looked last night while he was making sure I came a second time before he left. My stomach swirls in anticipation.

The contrast of the version of him standing here now with the boy I first met years ago makes me chuckle.

"Do you remember when you couldn't build a fire?"

He winks at me and steps a few feet out from our tent, crouching down to find the box of matches he probably set up earlier along with everything else.

"I could make a fire. I just wanted to see if *you* could make a fire. I wanted to watch you..." He flashes me a grin as he easily gets the kindling to flare up.

"You were so refined and proper, there is no way you knew how. I *taught* you how to be rough and tough."

"You, Josephine Wallace, taught me how to be a lot of things," he teases. His smile softens quickly. "You taught me how to be generous, and kind. And you taught me how to share, and want more than I'm supposed to—but," he stands and pulls me into his arms, and up next to his erection. "But I was always rough and tough."

"Oh, okay...sure, if that's what you want to believe."

He laughs. "And...yes, okay, fine Jojo. You taught me how to start a fire, but later I'll make you sorry for reminding me of it."

"Is that a promise or a threat?" I tease.

"A promising threat," he teases back with a wink. "Because I'm going to teach *you* some things tonight."

He chuckles, opening the cover on the portable fire pit to add a few larger logs on the top of what he's started. It crackles after a minute or two, the new logs catching instantly, and holding hands, we return to the tent.

"Happy Wedding Night, Mr. Sinclair." I give him a look that says how much I love him. He follows my every step with slow and steady ones of his own, his eyes growing suddenly hooded, his voice tentative and hesitant.

"I know you had the question when we said our vows. It was something we didn't address but I want you to know that you—you don't have to—you can stay *Mrs. Wallace*. My last name—maybe it's not right for you?" He lifts his chin, and I can tell he means it. I can read the worry in his eyes.

"How about we all—me, you and Emily—become Wallace-Sinclairs," I suggest. "We'll be hyphenated into a new name. A perfect union. The miracle union. So very hip."

"I love the sound of that. And yes, we are a miracle, the three of us." An expression of calm paints his face. It's like we both get there's a deeper, connective under- standing that comes with that word—a truth about us. Alex and I *are* a miracle. Emily even more so. We are the couple that shouldn't be, the forbidden family, star crossed, but instead of letting it ruin us, we simply persevered to fulfill our destiny.

We're true love. And we're married. And tonight means everything to me. To us.

His eyes lock on mine. I turn slowly so my back is to him and shoot him a look over my bare shoulders as I sweep my hair out of the way so the trail of buttons down my back is exposed.

"Mind helping me get this off?" I whisper huskily, while I bite at my lower lip. The warmth of his knuckles grazes my spine and the heat that's pulsing off of his body sends a shiver all the way down into my core.

I swallow hard. "I love you, Alex."

His lips fall gently against the back of my neck as his fingers trail along my back. His breath is close and hot against my tingling skin as he works the first button free.

ALEX

"I love you, too, Jojo. So much," I utter, dropping another kiss onto her soft nape while my fingers work quickly to unhook the next few of what has to be at least a hundred pearl buttons down the back of this dress. "I love you so much that I'm not going to rip this fucking dress off of you how I want to, because I know it's an antique and that it's your grandmother's...even though I want to."

She laughs, turning to send me a smirk. "Appreciated. *You...husband.*" The word, the look on her face, the way her voice shudders on the second syllable, undoes me. My hands start shaking, making my difficult task nearly impossible.

"Damn…did you have to call me *that*? It makes me sound so serious. Old!"

"It makes you sound hot."

"Too responsible," I laugh, tugging free a few more buttons, finally exposing the long expanse of her bare back and a sexy glimpse of a white, lacy bra with little sparkling things sewn onto it. My cock surges to life. "Let's see how you like being called…*wife.*"

"Oh. I like the sound of that."

"Do you?" I grin as she shivers and arcs her body towards me. I pause to run a finger along her spine, twining my finger into the back of her sexy bra strap, letting her know I've seen it, before returning to the infernal button job, because she knows and I know the only way through to seeing the front of this bra and what else she's wearing to turn me on is to exercise extreme, mind-blowing patience—one button at a time.

"Fuck." My fingers have accidentally tugged off two buttons too quickly and we've both heard the audible pop. I wince, watching the buttons disappear into the darkness outside my makeshift tent area. "I'm sorry, Jojo. We'll find them tomorrow."

"I think I can help." She reaches her hands around to the back and helps me undo the next few buttons that sit above her ass, but as she wiggles and moves closer to me, she's bumping into my cock and…*damn*…by the look on her face, I can tell that she knows she's not helping at all. She's nearly killing me.

"Yes!" I shout. Our hands meet at her lower back on

the last button. "You take it off because if I try, I'm going to shred it," I order, voice hoarse, body shaking with impatience.

I'm dropping my tux shirt and pants like they're on fire, and my dick is so heavy with want and need that I nearly blow it all when I turn to watch her gingerly working her way out of the sleeves then the bodice of the dress. The way she's stepping out of the rest of it is the best thing I've ever seen. Or at least, that's what I thought, until she unclasps this sexy sheer, fluffy and see-through slip thing that was under the dress and hiding the tiny piece of *lacy-what-the-fuck-sexy-floss* that runs up her perfect ass! This lacy nothing is now the best thing I've ever seen.

She reaches up to undo the pins in her hair so the circlet of flowers she's got up there can come off, but I beg her to stop. "Don't. Please leave it. Leave it all...Jojo, you're so sexy. Come over here."

"You come over here." She looks over at me, and my eyes follow how her hands are caressing her breasts over the fancy wedding bra that matches the thong.

Not needing a second invitation, I close the distance between us, and my mouth is on hers and I'm pushing her back into the mattress underneath all of the fancy bedding.

At first, I thought the mattress was too much, but now—the way I've torn that thong off of her, and I'm pounding into her—the way she's got her legs limp and spread wide for me as she's calling out my name half in whispers, half in moans, I'm happy I don't have to be careful or worry if I'm hurting her back.

"I know I promised not to rip any more panties, but...damn..."

"They weren't really panties, were they?" She finishes for me, tilting herself to meet my thrusts while her hands reach between us to push against me. I pause above her, locking eyes with her, wondering what she's about to do or if she's asking to stop, when she finds the weight of my cock and holds it in her hand. Grinning, she spreads her legs even wider, returning me to the opening of her fire-hot, wet clit.

"Just...feels so good..." I can barely form words as I enter her again. She bucks up in this sexy and involuntary jolt, moaning and biting that bottom lip of hers.

Suddenly, I'm so far in her, I swear I can feel the heat from the center of the earth pulsing into both of us. I'm so hard and she's so soft and slick—so sweet, accepting and loving. She moans for me to go faster and harder. I'm trying to keep the bulk of my weight off of her by leaning onto my forearms while her hands get tangled deep into my hair. She pulls kisses from my lips, and pants up and against my thrusts.

I come so hard I surprise myself, and by the way she's moaning and squeezing every inch of my cock with her pulsing body, I know for a fact she's coming hard, too. "Sorry—too fast, I know..." I mutter when our bodies have stopped throbbing and squeezing from explosions. "I had longer plans for how things were going to go inside this tent."

She squeezes her insides against me hard and presses her hands into my ass, grinning up into my face as if she enjoys how I gasp, jolt, and involuntarily thrust myself into her one last time while she pushes up to meet my movements. "Sorry for what? We have all night. And next time…I'm going to start on top—show you my own bigger and better plans."

I kiss her swollen lips, and when I try to pull out she holds me with a quick, "No. Stay in there. I want to feel you getting hard inside me."

I smile and flip her easily and without pulling out as commanded, so she's sitting up on top of me.

It takes only a few seconds staring up at her perfect tits, still encased in the white lacy bra, while she wiggles around on top of me to grow hard again.

"Wow. I can't believe you're already—"

I push up into her and she gasps out again, grinning. "Wow."

"A *husband* aims to please." I smile wickedly. "I did my part. Show me what you've got, *wife*."

15.

JOJO, PRESENT DAY.

I'm a *Mrs.* A wife. A very satisfied wife.

I keep bursting into smiles, even laughter, at that thought. And then I blush. I've never giggled so much, but I can't stop as I replay the memories of what this *Mrs. Wife* did with her *Mr. Husband* last night.

Alex and I couldn't wait to get back to Emily—to begin being a family. And Emily, being too little to understand what a honeymoon is supposed to be like, was going to be looking for us.

Like we were on some fancy honeymoon island and there were pretend servants waiting to clean it all up, we left the tent intact without a backward glance just before sunrise. Wrapped in the silk sheets, we only took the time to gather up my Grandmother's dress and Alex's tux before sneaking back to the house to shower before Emily, as if on cue, came skipping in looking for us to make her after-wedding-morning pancakes.

Despite our tiredness, we were both happy to be part of what we three declared officially as the newest Wallace-Sinclair tradition.

Alex has moved from using the boxed pancake mix to whipping up his own creations from scratch, always adding in chocolate chips. He says it's just at Emily's request, but I know—the chocolate chips are for him.

With full bellies, the four of us, plus the floppy, trouble-making Ajax, come out on to the deck. The wedding orchids we left scattered all over the rock yesterday have blown into the water. It's a rare day of clear, blue skies, something to be cherished around here.

"I want to swim!" Emily dances up to the water's edge putting her fingers in. "It's not too cold."

"I think it's too soon after eating. What do you think?" I turn to Alex, loving that I get to bring him into these simple decisions now. We're parents.

"I think it's colder than you imagine, Emily." Alex shudders, joining Emily at the water. "But." He wiggles his brows and starts rolling up his pants. "It's not too soon to wade in and learn how to skip rocks."

Laughing, Emily splashes her feet into the water, watching carefully and then copying Alex's demonstrations of how to skip a rock. Her fingers are still too small and maybe a bit uncoordinated to get the perfect flick on a stone.

"Show me one more time, Daddy," she begs Alex, as though she's called him Daddy since the day she was born.

"You pick the rock this time," my *husband—Emily's daddy*—responds, both of those words filling me up with as much brightness as the sun.

Emily finds a heavy one that won't skip at all, so when she's distracted, Alex switches it out for something a little flatter. He bends his elbow and tells her to watch just as he's releasing the stone across the water.

"One...two...three, four, five...six!" Emily counts every fast-bounce the rock makes along the glassy surface, ringlets of broken water mark each touch, as if the water is keeping score.

"That's the most skips yet!" She leaps into Alex's arms, and this time, he walks with her deeper into the water, ready in case she tries to go too deep.

I move closer to them, cooling my feet in the lake along with them, and I groan at my family as they give up on throwing rocks to turn and splash me.

Aunt Shelly pulls her shoes from her feet eventually and joins me. "I'm so happy for you, dear," she says quietly. "So happy."

Before I can hug my aunt or even respond, Alex's phone starts to blare from our pile of things back on dry land, so he takes Emily's hand and leads her back to me, pausing to kiss me on the lips before jogging up to answer the phone. Curious, I do my best to listen, but I'm not able to make out Alex's words. I wonder if it's May, but also hope it's Grady.

Last night, Alex told me he'd spoken with May before the wedding. He also told me that May didn't deny murdering his father, and he admitted that he was maybe okay with his mother's actions, if they were true. I admitted that I also was okay with it, and then for an entire hour we stared up at the stars questioning ourselves, asking if we were now bad people.

Alex and I never came to a final answer to that question. Good or bad, we both felt how we felt about Michael Sinclair being dead.

Good. Safe. Justified. And as always…somehow, sad.

As for May? As much as I have cursed that woman for never standing up for Alex, somehow the knowledge that she is aware we're married now—and that maybe she did kill Michael Sinclair to finally save her sons from more future torture—all oddly puts my heart at ease.

Alex also said he was worried about her. He said she seemed a little scattered and paranoid yesterday and maybe was starting to break, like some sort of PTSD as she grapples with no longer being tied to his father. He said she looked and acted so strangely yesterday, and he also cautioned me to still treat her as a threat. Until he can know anything for certain, and at least until our business is settled with Grady, I promised I would be cautious.

We both agreed to leave our suspicions about Michael Sinclair's murderer alone, and we also decided to give May time. We would leave town without engaging her at all and simply wait. Time heals all, people say, and in the case of poor May, I hope the saying can be as true for her as it will be for me and Alex.

I'm so focused on Alex's phone call that when he starts nodding at me and mouthing the word "Grady" along with giving me a huge thumbs up, I rest at ease and turn my attention to the water below. Even with our splashing, the fish have gathered close. Nothing big like when you sneak up on them. These are Olympic Mudminnows, fish we could use to catch other fish. Emily would love them. I follow one that's darting close to us, and I memorize his pattern, the way he kisses at the stones nearby and avoids the others. I hold my breath and grin a second before my hands plunge into the water, cupping the creature and bringing his little, flailing body up in my palms.

"You caught him! Show me! Show me!" Emily jumps on her toes, so I kneel lower to give her a view of the fish. It's so tiny I'm able to dip my palms back down into the water, providing it a small pool so he can breathe easily.

"That's how your mom used to catch all of the fish." Alex is suddenly behind me.

"Mom, you're amazing!" My chest swells hearing my daughter praise me.

"Yes, she is," Alex echoes, and my heart pumps even more.

I let the fish go gently then let Emily try to catch some on her own, making her promise to stay within my reach.

"Grady accepted my offer," Alex says as soon as our eyes meet. As if I've been holding my breath for days, I exhale heavily and fall into his hug.

"Of course he did," I say, quivering with relief. "Oh my God...that's it then. You sign it all over and we're free to just walk away from here."

"Yes. We're free." His eyes move to the horizon.

"No regrets, right?" I ask.

"None."

I stand in his arms, swaying side-to-side and relishing this feeling while Emily splashes around our legs, driving fish away with her loud and unabashed style. We both begin to laugh, and our daughter gives up on fishing and runs wild up the shore pathway where her barking puppy has raced up the hill.

Alex and I rush up the shore after her, and soon Aunt Shelly joins in when the puppy rushes off with one of her flip-flops.

It's hard to say how long May was standing on the trail, looking down, watching us. We were all so distracted with our own happiness that we simply never saw her. Nobody expected her to be there.

"Hello. Who are you?" I hear Emily ask. My throat goes dry with panic as I try to speed up my pace without looking scary or hysterical, because that's how I feel.

"I—only just heard about you so I had to come see for myself. I'm your Grandmother. Your daddy's mother," she says, her eyes fixed wide and glazed on Emily.

As I get closer, I try to analyze May's face. Like Alex said, she doesn't look right. Her hair is all askew, which is not like her at all. She's never the kind to let one strand out of place, and I could swear to God that under her makeup she's got...*dirt? Or...bruises?* Grady has carried on the abuse.

My heart starts to pound wildly and the tips of my fingers grow numb from wanting to snatch Emily away from the woman, while fear crawls up my veins, my neck, my throat, until I can't speak.

"Alex!" His name finally bursts from my lungs. I don't dare take my eyes off of my daughter, who is stopped halfway between me and the woman who has been stalking me—*us.* I'm sure it's only seconds but it feels like an eternity before his voice calls back in response and his weight is behind me.

"Emily, come here love." He calls out to her, stepping in front of me.

Our daughter, ever fearless, doesn't listen.

"This is my *grandmother*, Daddy," she calls back, voice full of wonder and joy. "I didn't even know I had a grandmother and I always wanted one; did you know that?"

Her steps aren't even cautious as her head tilts and she moves closer to get a better look at this woman who I have desperately tried to keep a mystery to her.

"You have eyes just like me and daddy," Emily says to May.

"Yes," May chokes out. "Exactly." May's body shakes

once, a gulp falling from her lips as her eyes begin to gloss with tears.

"We are really a big family now," Emily says, stepping closer and reaching out her hand. Alex's entire body grows tense.

I don't know why I do it—why this sudden feeling of hope and trust takes hold of me—but I jut my arm out to the side halting him and I whisper, "wait."

Emily reaches out more until May's hand lifts and connects with hers—fingertips pressed together as if they're looking through a mirror.

"I'm so happy to meet you…"

"My name's Emily," my daughter helps her finish the sentence.

"Emily," May repeats, her lips shivering like she might cry.

"And I can call you Granny. Or Gran. Or Nana. That's what my friend calls her grandmother. Nana. It sounds really nice to me—*Nana*."

"Does it? Then you may call me Nana, if you'd like to," May whispers out.

"I'd like to. *Nana*." Emily shouts the word gleefully, unaware of every bad implication of this relationship. She only sees the good, and so she flings herself into May's arms and gives her a hug. "My Nana!"

When May flicks her gaze to me and Alex, I can read the wonder and sweetness in her expression. It's like Emily is such a surprise to her—like she'd never thought she would have this. As her arms go around Emily's slight form, I can almost hear her processing it all. That she has *a granddaughter.* One that loves her unconditionally. A child that came to her as a surprise, but that is very much like her. A child that appeared without rules and constrictions applied to how May's supposed to treat her. A child with no threats or dangers already hung over her head, coming from a husband who would dictate just how much May was allowed to love.

Please let Emily change her—heal her, I think and I pray. *Please let this be okay.*

"She's beautiful," May says as Emily steps out of the hug, and her hands go over Emily's long curls. Our daughter slips her hand into May's and holds it tight, beaming at all of us. It's the smallest gesture, and I'm watching May's face as it melts and then seems to crumple as the softness in her face returns to hard.

"Emily." I call out, my voice stern. "Can you go chase after Ajax and put him in the house? He's running away, and you know Aunt Shelly can't run as fast as you."

Alex, who must have noticed what I did, steps in quickly, his hand grabbing our daughter's away from May's. He lifts her away from what still feels like a warning and sends her down the pathway to where Shelly's been watching everything unfold.

"Okay! Be right back, Nana. She should stay for dinner. Stay and play!" Emily grins back over her shoulder at her new-found grandmother then skips off down the pathway.

I share a glance and a nod with Shelly that communicates "get Emily inside, and do not let her come back out of the house." Shelly nods back, understanding.

"I'm happy I met her, Alex, but something like this—like a daughter—should not have been kept secret. If I had known, I could have done...something. Don't you see? I could have tried to...maybe...somehow..." May starts crying.

"I only just found out about her myself, Mother," Alex answers gently, his tone somewhere between sorry and cautious.

"I didn't tell him. Not anyone," I add, saddened at May's complete and obvious upset over this.

"But my husband—he—" she whispers through tears.

"Let's not bring him up, Mom. I would like to think that Father would have softened about her, just how you did."

May shakes her head, because we all know Michael Sinclair would not have softened over Emily. Not one bit. May goes on muttering, "I just realized he probably knew all along—which is why—oh, God. And now there's not time..."

"Mother." Alex steps forward. "There is time. All of the time in the world. You will get to know her and she you. You're her Nana now. We won't keep her from you. I promise you that."

"No." May shakes her head, and I see her hands trembling wildly. "There's not time, and it's still very dangerous for you, Alex. More than I thought. The business—the oil." She points at the lake. "And the water.

What you did Alex. What you did—the secrets you kept from all of us for so long. It's so huge. It's too much, and he's really, really angry."

That irrational panic that Alex told me May had displayed before starts to become apparent. She's twisting her hands in front of her and her eyes are darting around the landscape as if she's waiting for a bad guy to pop out from hiding and shove her in a van or something. "I need you to go now. I need you to take that little girl right now, in your car, and drive away from here. Fast."

"We're just waiting to finalize things with Grady," Alex explains. "He finally called me, and we plan to settle things tonight. I'm giving him the oil and the water, and even this damn house if he wants it. And by the weekend, we'll be gone from here. It's going to be fine. All is falling into place."

"Grady…he's not to be trusted. I tried to get through to him, but you need to watch your back with him, Alex. He has always followed your father's plans—always been trying to screw you over, but you know that, don't you?"

I know Alex spoke to her about our plans, about giving Grady what he wants so we can be free to leave. This is the first I've heard about him giving away the lake house, but fine. If that's what it takes, then fine. I don't care. Alex and I will find another lake to love. But May's making it sound as if we need to flee impending doom—today. My convictions and suspicions about May murdering Mr. Sinclair fall away.

This frightened, scattered woman doesn't seem capable of shooting her husband in broad daylight. She doesn't seem capable of holding a gun in her hand at all, and I start to wonder if she's not warning us away from Grady. Because how else would May have gotten bruises?

She seems terrified, and my mind immediately goes to thoughts of her being afraid of Grady hurting Alex. Does she foresee him betraying Alex in the middle of this deal they're meant to sign? My chest floods with panic. *Like father like son*; is that what's going on?

"Yes, Mother. I know that, and I don't care this time. I mean to sign everything he puts in front of me. I won't fight him on any of it."

"You don't have time for that—for deals and paperwork. You have to leave—today, Alex." May locks gazes with me, pleading. "All of you, Jojo. Today."

Her cell phone buzzes in her pocket, and her eyes grow wild as she pulls it out and hangs up on whomever was calling her. "I have to go or there will be more trouble. I'm so happy I got to meet Emily. Please tell her I said goodbye. Tell her I'll try to make this better, but between us, I don't think I can," she whispers out, crying openly now as she backs away. "I'm sorry, Alex. I'm so sorry. I didn't understand…"

Alex reaches for his mom again, but she turns and heads toward where she's parked her car in the upper driveway.

"Do you think she's going to be okay? Did you see

her bruises?" I'm hoping Alex will somehow be able to explain it away for me.

"Yes," he says, staring at her back as she rushes away.

"And do you think—?"

"Grady. The motherfucker. I will draw up a new contract that says he's not allowed to touch her or interact with her ever again, or the deal is off." Alex's breathing has grown rapid and angry, his body boiling.

"Do you think you can do that? Keep him away from her?"

"Why not? It's only one more person he has to avoid. I think he'll avoid the world if he gets all of the riches," Alex answers with complete confidence, as mine slips away more. But I don't shout out what my mind, and a new wave of paranoia, is screaming at me. *Is all of this just for show? Is Grady going to hurt Alex, and May, and me and Emily? Are we walking into a trap? Are we being stupid? Now that May's seen Emily, why do I feel so afraid, more afraid than ever before?*

Alex shakes his head, sighing. "This has to be some sort of PTSD Mother's having. I will get her to see a therapist before we go away. She needs to talk to someone. Maybe some antidepressants? Hell, I don't know, CBD or pot or whatever…but she's not okay."

I let go of her as Alex steps back up to my side and pushes his phone into the damp pocket of his shorts.

"Grady's texting. He's ready. He said to meet at my building—at my place." Alex shows me the phone as the next text comes in from Grady with, "Correction, Bro.

Let's meet at *MY NEW PENTHOUSE*. I'm going to be moving in today, so bring some duffle bags to take out anything you might want. Tomorrow the lock codes and the keys will be changed."

Alex smiles at that, breathing in a huge sigh of relief.

"A good sign. He's obviously all in, right? Guy thinks I'm devastated about giving up that building, but I never even liked that place. Never. Just rehabbed that building and stayed there to please Father. I told him he could even have my clothes in the closet. He loved that idea. Fucking greedy bastard. He always wanted to be me. My suits will never fit his ass."

His calm and cynicism washes away some of my worries, but only some as my mind swirls with hundreds of new scenarios. There is no way I can trust Grady now. Not after what May said, not after the bruising on her face. I've got this huge gut feeling that we need to hide Emily—hide her now until we've faced Grady and gotten through this next step.

"I'm coming with you."

He starts shaking his head, but I keep talking before he can protest more. "Alex, I'm seriously coming with you. We're going to drive Shelly, Ajax and Emily over to your Father's hunting cottage where they will stay hidden. I want to give her instructions that if she doesn't hear from us, she's to run. In the meantime, Shelly will make it a game. We'll tell Emily that they're going to an amazing playhouse, while you and I face down the final dragon together. I'll make sure you don't lose your temper—and together, we will get through this. Now that your mom's seen Emily, you know we can't leave them here alone without hiding them, and you also know it's a bad idea to take them all with us."

"I think you're overreacting." He sighs, but when his eyes meet mine, he sees my resolve.

"I think you're right there with me, Alex. Stop bull-shitting me. You're afraid, too."

He breathes out again, long and loud, and his mask slips just enough to where I can see I'm right.

"I am," he grits out. "I want to hide both you and Emily. I want to drive the hell away from here just how my mother told us to do. But we need to face Grady. We need to close this properly or we'll always be looking over our shoulders."

I nod, satisfied. "I agree. You tell Shelly what's up, and I'll go pack up some things for Emily."

16.

JOJO, PRESENT DAY.

I'm glad I came with him.

We could hear Grady talking to himself from Alex's office the moment we got off the elevator and walked into the foyer. He's repeating something about how wronged he always is—something about everything being *unfair*, which makes me think he's reading through the papers Alex's lawyers had emailed over. For Grady, everything has always been unfair. This "unjust life" is what fuels him. It used to make me so angry to hear him say it, because he has always been so cruel. But now I see how the monster he is was made. He made terrible choices, but they weren't all his to make.

I check my phone while Alex makes a big show of coughing and being noisy so as not to *surprise* Grady. We don't want to set him off by making him think we were eavesdropping. He loudly knocks on the office door, calling out "Grady?"

I'm relieved when I finally get a text from Aunt Shelly with photos that show how she and Emily are having fun at the Sinclair's hunting lodge. Alex and I went through the whole place, checking rooms and the outbuildings for signs of May or anything out of the ordinary, but from the looks of the place, it had been closed up for more than five years. Probably the last time Mr. Sinclair had the energy or the time to go hunting.

Shelly's next batch of texts come in a sort of code her and I developed. She lets me know that she's put the fruit in the bedroom in case they need snacks. That means she has the gun I sent with her tucked away safely, but ready for an emergency.

Walt is coming to join them because his hunting campsite is only two miles to the south. Shelly says she told him about May and all of her crazy behavior, and he felt it was best that he was with them just in case. Shelly's as nervous as I am now. I can sense it in her hurried mountain of texts. Walt promised to be there by sunset, which gives me an extra layer of calm.

My phone bings with one last notice, and it's a picture of Emily grinning, holding a puzzle and swinging her feet from the cool loft inside the lodge. I laugh quietly to myself because she's so darn cute, but the lighthearted feeling flees the second Grady opens the office door.

"Why did you bring *her?*" Grady asks, frowning.

"As my wife, she's going to have to sign everything too."

Grady's eyes widen at that word, but he manages to keep his own poker face intact as he nods. "Fine. Come in."

I tuck my phone in my purse, pull my bag close to my body, and remind myself that I have Alex's gun in here. I also repeat in my head my promise to not let either of us use it. If one of us has to, though, it needs to be me, which is why I'm in charge of it. Alex can't have any trouble. I could prove that it was self-defense a lot easier than he could.

"Let's get this over with, *thief*," Grady says through gritted teeth as he sits in the large desk chair and motions us to the two leather ones on the opposite side of the mahogany table. It's strange to have him acting like he's the host when technically, Alex still owns this place.

"Thief, huh? Really?" Alex stares at his brother for a second, so I touch his hand with the back of mine to remind him why we're here. He can't let his brother push him into acting out. He finally sighs.

"Yeah, you're a thief. All of this should have been mine to begin with but you stole it, just like you stole Father away from me."

Alex blinks at his brother, who is shifty with his movements and unsettled in his own skin. He seems high, and I wonder if maybe he is. Grady's been drunk around me plenty, and a drug habit wouldn't shock me at all.

"Grady, I meant what I said. I *want* you to have this with my whole heart. You know I didn't steal anything— the will...it was Father's last way of fucking with us. That document was his last way of tearing us apart so we couldn't ever be brothers. Can't you see that? He never wanted us to have a relationship," Alex says, and my heart swells because my Alex, he's so sincere. He's so generous and hopeful for change—a real change—even now. I have great doubts it will happen. I just don't think it's possible.

"You were the eldest," Alex continues, stroking Grady's ego. "Tradition dictates the eldest son should be heir, and there is no argument that you were always the best and most loyal Sinclair."

"Damn right I was, and I still am." Grady puffs up his chest, while Alex only seems to deflate and look sad.

"You know I don't have what it takes to fill Father's shoes how he wanted me to," Alex admits. We practiced this part during our drive, and it's coming out so honestly. I think there's a sliver inside of him that always wanted to make his father proud and hates that he never did.

"Nice to hear you say it out loud." Grady smirks.

"I like to think you also don't have what it takes. That you'll be a better man than Father was. That you will work to end the darkness." Alex scoots forward in his chair, dialing in on Grady's gaze, trying to reach him.

"Brother. Why the hell not? We can be family—*real* brothers. We're all each other's got."

"We're fucked up brothers in a fucked up family. I don't see any of that changing." There's a harsh swallow that chokes Grady after those words come cascading out.

Alex blinks.

"We don't have to be; we're in control now. You—you're going to be in control now." He corrects himself. "And we can fix all of this shit—the past...hell, the future too. We can start over. We can work towards knowing and understanding each other."

Alex leans in, eyes pleading. "I saw some bruises on Mother's face. She tried to cover them up with makeup. Please tell me they're not from you—please tell me I didn't see what I saw. She was acting like she's losing it, just like how she used to be in the past, when we were little, and I just need to know that you didn't have anything to do with that."

His voice is low, non-threatening and sad.

"Bruises? On Mother? I wouldn't hit her—no! I—*fuck* —how bad was it?" His face grows pale, his eyes go wide —wild, like he, too, is suddenly afraid. Alex shares a look with me, and I shrug, because for once in my life I actually believe Grady's response. He didn't do it, so maybe May fell or hurt herself intentionally. Maybe she did it to herself to work her way in and buy sympathy. I don't put anything past this family.

"Where is she now? Did she come see you?" Grady's voice is tinged with panic.

"Yes. She did, but I didn't have time to really observe much of her before she rushed off saying she was late. I've seen her a couple of times now, and Mother truly seems off." Alex shakes his head, clearly confused at how Grady's responding—like he's truly upset. He was so sure his brother was the one to cause this behavior in May. So was I.

"The bruises just shook me up, that's all." Alex points at my face next. "It took Jojo weeks to heal up from what you did to her."

"And it took me a month to heal from what you did to me," Grady says, voice shaking. My stomach begins a low boil hearing my injuries brought into the discussion, especially with Grady's complete lack of remorse. Like I said, *always unfair*.

Alex opens his mouth to respond, but Grady holds up his hands, his eyes drifting to me as he speaks fast. "Wait...before we sign any of this shit..."

Grady stalls for a few seconds, his gaze wandering off to the side as he blinks. His head cocks as his focus shifts to me, and when his heavy stare remains on my face for more than a full breath, I grow hot. What starts as fear and shifts to anger begins to resolve into pity, though. His throat moves with a sharp swallow, and his mouth twitches, lips quivering nervously.

"I want to say straight up, Jojo—Alex." His voice drops to a low hum and his face shifts into an uncomfortable seriousness, as if he's pushing himself to walk through a fire but maintain his bravery despite how badly it hurts. "I *need* to say this. I'm...sorry I hurt you, Jojo. I truly am. Now that I've had time to process everything, I just want you to know that was unnecessary, and now—*today*—I see how it's all getting so fucked up. I feel bad about it. I do have a conscience, you know? I do."

His gaze dips to the top of the desk for a moment, and when he looks at me again, I swear to God I see, for the very first time in his eyes, what looks like regret. There's self-hatred brewing in those eyes. The monster is realizing what he is, and maybe how he was made.

I nod, but don't say anything as Alex fills the crackling air in the room with his own apologies to his brother.

"I'm sorry too, Grady. We need to remember that we were kids, forced into a horrible position. We were made to become people we didn't recognize, people who didn't know how to rebel against their father's twisted goals. I'm also sorry we had a mother who was so abused she couldn't fight for us. But now..." Alex wavers, glancing at me. "With father gone, I'm clear, and I hope you can get clear too. I'm happy to give everything back to you. In time, I want a relationship with you, Grady. A *real* one. I'm serious. We just have to agree to not hurt each other anymore. If we can shake off the ties that bound us, we can make new ones. I know we can be brothers. We can protect our family, and we can protect what Father left behind for us—*for you*. All for you now."

He gives Grady a meaningful look. "The land, the oil —and the water—it's a huge responsibility to take on, and I want you to know I'm available anytime should you want advice. If you want any sort of help, I am at your disposal, with the ultimate decision always being yours...of course. I'm leaving Tacoma to start my own life, but I'm always going to be here." He places a hand over his heart.

My chest twists at the earnestness and longing that crosses Alex's face. My soul hurts for him then loves him so deeply all at once. My lungs can hardly pull in air. Because even though Alex swore he was finished with Grady—with this place and his family—at the eleventh hour, he can't resist his true essence.

He's always been the kind-hearted, loving, and generous boy who only wanted a family to love him back.

True to *his own* essence, Grady's eyes grow dark as he answers, "What about the lake? You're giving me the lake—the house and the lake?"

Alex's shoulders slump in defeat as he nods. "That's why I let Jojo come here with me. The house, yes. No problem. I've got the papers for that drawn up, but the lake." He looks at me then. "Half of the entire lake, and the aquifer underneath, belongs to *her*—and it always has. Here, Jojo. Please come look."

Motioning me away from the windows, Alex pulls a

stack of legal papers out of his messenger bag and sets them in front of Grady. He reaches in, and from the slim front pocket pulls out a yellowed, crumpled paper as well. When I notice that it's a deed, just like the deeds and trusts I was looking at inside the county building the days following Michael Sinclair's funeral, my heart begins a slow, dreadful thumping.

"What is this?" I ask him.

"It's the original deed to the lake. It's my apology. It's my redemption." Alex smoothes it as flat as it will go on top of the desk, and waits for Grady and I to crowd around and read. Grady gasps as my hands go over my heart and my eyes tear up as I note it's dated the same night my father died. He gave me the lake. His lake.

His apology for a crime that wasn't his fault.

"I can't believe you did this. Utter...hardcore...family betrayal! No wonder Father went so insane," Grady growls in a whisper, shocked. He blocks my view of it as he reads the deed for himself.

All I can think about is how so many people have given this lake away—even my mother.

"Father never knew I gave half of the lake to Jojo," Alex tells Grady, sounding half-proud, half-defensive while I reel with shock, absorbing the ramifications of this act.

Alex signed over half of what is easily the most important piece of land in the Sinclair fold to me. But how? When?

"How do you *know* Father never knew? I'll bet he

knew. You always act so sure of yourself when you're full of shit."

Grady turns back and locks eyes with Alex. For some reason the odd-smirk on Grady's face makes my stomach churn with dread.

Alex's expression is clear and confident as he replies, "I'm still *alive*, Grady. That's how I know."

Grady nods, but his usual asshole-smirk falls off of his face when Alex explains more, "I owed the lake to Jojo, Grady. We all did. We took her father away when her mother was dying from cancer. We tortured her, made her cry, messed with her head. She was innocent, and we made her become part of a feud that had nothing to do with her. You get that, right? We were brutal. It was a fair trade."

"How can you say she's not part of the feud?" Grady shouts. "She's a damn Wallace girl. Through and through." He scoffs out, "*Fair.* What does that word mean to us, Alex? Being born Michael Sinclair's son—is that fucking fair?"

"No. It wasn't," Alex answers simply. "But we aren't that anymore, are we? He's gone, and now we can finally be brothers."

"Fuck you, Alex. Stop saying that to me. You sound like a sentimental sappy asshole. Endangering all of us, and fucking up our lives even more all because of your damn *lake-gift* and for—"

"For *love*. For family." Alex stops Grady's tirade while he reaches over and picks up my hand. "For a love and a new kind of family that I hope includes you one day. If you'll let it," Alex adds.

"Just like that stupid word fair, *brother*," Grady bites out, shooting me an icy glare and taking his anger, along with something I can't define, out at me. "We don't get to have family or love or be that kind of brother to each other. It's fucking impossible."

"You're wrong, Grady," Alex insists. "We can have it. We will have it, and even though I know we have miles to go between us, and some fucked up, dark as hell water under our bridge, I'll just lay the word down at your feet. I love you because you're my brother. I always have, Grady."

"You're mental." Grady shakes his head and turns back to the deed, continuing to utter low, but markedly less angry curses. His facade has cracks forming.

Alex's eyes delve deep and search into mine. "Father —*our father.*" He motions to include Grady in what he's saying. "He also made Grady participate in your Father's murder."

"I *know* Alex. I know and I've forgiven you, and you don't have to revisit that." I don't want to hear it— picture it--die inside all over again.

"I want you to forgive Grady, too," Alex whispers. "He needs to hear it."

His words make my body hurt, because I wonder if I'm capable of forgiving Grady. This ask...it's too big. I would give my husband anything, but this? Why does he ask this?

His words also cause Grady to pull in a fast breath and turn to face me again. Grady's eyes are hooded and oddly stained with what might be a hint of...hope? Alex quietly moves into our shared memories and utters words that hurt, that I do not want to hear, or live through ever again.

"Grady went home before your father died, and—as you know—I was on the opposite walkway from where it all happened, unable to help."

I nod once, trying to keep it together.

"Grady did just as much horrible shit as I did that day—and before—and after."

"And always," I accuse.

Alex doesn't deny it, he simply nods once too. "Grady—he had been cast as the villain in the narrative our father had orchestrated for years and years. Ever since we were little, I got to play the good guy. The smart kid. Grady—he was the bad guy. But none of it was true. Grady and I, though we weren't ever allowed to say it, he and I were actually the same. I was as horrible as he was to you, Jojo. Maybe worse because at least Grady was out in the open while I was lying."

"You—weren't—" I start, but he stops me by holding up a shaking hand.

"We were both playing our parts, and following Father's orders. Grady had to hold a gun to my head and threaten to kill me if I didn't follow him to your farm. He was still recovering from his surgery. A surgery our father paid for after he was the one who had beaten and destroyed Grady's football-throwing arm. We were both living with horrendous abuse. Each day was a pressure cooker, trapped in a vice that turned and turned on us until it broke us, over and over again. I think now, looking back, that Father would do it so he could fit us back together—rebuild us as he saw fit for his plans, and then when those changed, he'd do it to us again. Me, I was lucky. My torture was mostly fear based. Fear that *you* would be hurt always kept me in line. And maybe because I was smaller, Father didn't beat me so often because he was concerned people would find out. He hit Grady a lot more, because Grady was stronger. Because he could take it. By the year your father was murdered, my brother had been so physically and mentally abused he'd made it through his own type of rebellion against father, and I, at that time was totally oblivious to what he was going through. I wasn't there for you Grady, and I'm sorry about that."

Grady doesn't answer. His eyes are cold, shattered —closed off.

My gaze ricochets between Alex and Grady, between these brothers, and suddenly I'm finding it nearly impossible to imagine that Grady had once tried to *rebel* against Michael Sinclair. Even though I don't want to hear more, mostly because I don't want to see Grady as anything but a monster because that's what he's always been to me, I find my own heart cracking for him as I whisper in shock, "Grady? What…did he do?"

Grady still doesn't answer; he simply looks away

from both of us, tensing up his whole body as if bringing up this story is hurting him as much as it hurts for me to think about my father's death again.

Alex goes on, eyes only on me. "My brother had huge dreams. He was the best quarterback our school—no... hell...our town and whole region—ever had. Recruiters had noticed, and all on his own Grady had landed more than one full-ride scholarship to some top universities. He'd had his choice of any Big Six school he'd wanted, and he'd gone into it thinking our father would be proud of him for saving the family money, so he'd kept the scholarships as a surprise. But Father didn't want Grady playing in the Big Six. He didn't want any chances of Grady or I getting out of Tacoma and out of the family business. Quarterbacks like Grady play for the NFL, and they get to have their own money and be free from the noose Father had kept nice and tight around our necks. So, instead, *good-ole Dad* beat his dreams away. Literally beat him with a crowbar to make sure the arm was irreparable."

I pull in a breath, my hands going over my heart. "No."

Alex nods, and I can see Grady's shoulders slumping and shaking. "Despite the story about Grady's 'injury' in the Tacoma news, and the police backing the story too, there was no car accident that messed up my brother." He barks out a sharp, pained laugh. "Fuck. My father... he invented the concept of 'fake news' long before it was trendy."

"I don't want people feeling sorry for me."

"She's not people, Grady. She's Jojo," Alex whispers. "And she needs to know it all."

Grady's now paced back and forth to the windows. He's grabbed his shoulder, and when he turns back to us, his face is contorting as he's trying to keep his mask in place as Alex relentlessly finishes the tale. "Anyhow... now you know some of Grady's side of the pain. But Jojo...what I've told you? The arm—it doesn't scratch the surface of the mountains of shit and beatings, and other pain that Grady and I have buried deep inside of us. We'll both be fucked up from it forever." He shrugs. "But yeah, in my mind, I won't give up on us, Grady. Even though we weren't allowed to be, we were and still are brothers. Real ones. And that means a lot to me. I hope it can mean something to you, too."

Alex coughs then and stops talking like maybe his throat is closing up from a wave of tears.

My stomach has dropped, and my own tears now threaten at the edges of my eyes as I look at Grady's shocked and pain-filled eyes. I imagine him how he looked—acted—back in high school. He'd always been so angry and hateful. Endlessly cruel. But I also remember the big 'car-accident' reports that were in our newspaper. On our local TV station, too. How the town had gossiped about it—how everyone, even his own father, had said it was such a terrible tragedy that *his dear boy* was robbed of his natural talent. I also remember exactly when Grady had gone through that surgery. I suppose Grady's father had made him go sit on the bench for the rest of the entire season, because that's where he'd been. The injured kid, cheering his team on from the sidelines. Each game must have broken his soul, and Michael Sinclair must have loved watching every minute of it.

Poor Grady...following his father's orders...hating me, hating Alex...hating his whole life...

"I'm sorry Grady." I blurt out. "I didn't know," I whisper after the silence between us has stretched too long. I suppose, despite what he's done to me, past and present, I *am* truly sorry for the life he was forced to live. And though the next words fall more slowly out of my mouth and are difficult to form, I find they aren't impossible. "I'm angry at you still. Very. And I will be for a long, long time." I pull in a shaking breath. "But for Alex, and for my own healing...and for yours," I shudder, wondering if any of us ever will be truly healed, "I will try—I mean—I do—*I do* forgive you."

A few tears sneak out and trail down my cheeks for him, for Alex, for me. For my father and mother, too.

Grady, as though he can't even believe what I've just said to him, shakes his head and rips his eyes away from mine. I register a look that says either he doesn't believe me or, maybe, he doesn't think he deserves the words I've said.

"We were all just trying to survive," Alex chokes out, finally able to speak again. He places an arm around me and squeezes my shoulder, whispering a fast and quiet, "thank you" into my ear before adding, "When your Father died, and I was helpless to do anything but shout my promises to him about how I'd be there for you, at the same time, Grady was already home with Father. He was getting another massive beating for taking too long to pick me up after school. Even though Grady had done everything right and we were exactly on schedule as ordered, Grady got beat so badly he had to miss a couple days of school. Father was endlessly doing that shit to him, making Grady hate me and blame me for these beatings."

I shake my head, once again trying to walk in Grady's fucked-up shoes. I'd processed the new details of my father's murder when Alex came clean to me, and even though I know the facts about how he died—and even though my own mother told me that she was very sure Mr. Sinclair *murdered* my father long before Alex admitted his part in it—having to look at the entire scenario from Grady's point of view rips open all of the old wounds in an unexpected, raw and horrible way.

"How could someone do this their own children?" I shake my head, feeling a new flood of pain. This new perspective makes me momentarily, irrationally and incorrectly angry at *Alex* in a way I've never felt.

It makes the old questions I never asked Alex come burning up inside my chest. *Why didn't Alex try harder? Why didn't he just let Grady shoot him with that gun instead of participating in his Father's horrible 'orders' how he did? I know I'd rather die than kill someone as good and as nice as my father. How could he just sit back and watch it all unfold, watch my father sink and suffocate in the grain like that? Why? How could he love me and also keep these huge secrets from me year after year?*

My anger dissipates as quickly as it comes while I watch the two brothers meet gazes.

They'd suffered so much.

Their tortured expressions seem to war with each other. Alex's is all about the future full of possible openness and hope. Grady's is locked in the past—still dark and wounded. I watch both expressions crumble as they seem to be remembering and questioning their own endless tirade of *why* along with mine.

All these years, it's been about survival. As for Alex, I at least have the answer to my questions. It's been about keeping me alive. He did what he did—good and bad, right and so wrong—to keep me breathing.

"After Mr. Wallace died, I became a good Sinclair. And I was. Wasn't I, Grady?" Alex's voice is a whisper. "We both became very good. Better than ever. I never bothered you again. Never got you in trouble again. Was never resistant to any new orders, not once I knew how much it hurt you if I balked."

Alex's body is shaking hard, but he doesn't cry. His eyes stay focused on Grady, who nods his answer. Any new light that was flickering there suddenly goes back to flat. Dead. Grady's got his mask back on tight, and his expression reminds me way too much of their father's.

He picks up the deed to the lake. "But you signed this

paper." His voice crackles. "You kept this secret from me and Father—so you weren't being good, you were...cheating."

"It was my one rebellion, Grady. Like yours." Alex shrugs while he takes the document from Grady. His fingers smooth the edges of the crumpled paper, and then pause where my signature is written—where I know Alex perfectly *forged* my signature. "This deed saved me. I could only be a part of Father's feud because I knew that deep down Jojo had been gifted half of what I loved the most. The lake. It was stupid, and yes, it was dangerous. But it's what saved my soul. I needed one good thing in the middle of all of the bad. Please understand."

Grady pushes away from his desk and starts pacing the room, running his hands through his thick hair. "You know he'd kill you right here and kill you now if he could *hear* the shit falling out of your mouth? He'd peel the skin off of your body and smile while you screamed. You know that, right?"

"Oh, I know." Alex barks out another heavy, bitter laugh. "Let's be real, bro. Father would have made *you* peel the skin off my body. Made *you* clean up the mess it would make, and he'd not smile—he'd laugh in both of our faces the whole time."

"Fuck. Touché." Grady shudders at that, a sad, desolate smile curves on his lips, because Alex's portrayal is dead on. "Where was this original deed kept this whole time?" Grady whispers.

"I stashed it in the lining of my school backpack. Sewed it inside, and kept it there until I pulled it out to come here. Jojo and I will sign it over to you along with everything else."

He turns to me, eyes pleading. "I should have told you about this gift long ago—at least when you showed up in town for the funeral—and for sure I should have told you after our wedding, but for some reason I was afraid to, Jojo."

"You're actually fucking married." Grady's eyes go distant. "And you had a...a wedding? What the fuck?"

"Did you expect anything else?" Alex takes up my left hand and holds it up so he can show the rings. "We filed officially with the city online yesterday. She's now Jojo Wallace-Sinclair, and I'm Alex Wallace-Sincliar. A new family name. United."

"Holy...*fuck*. What have you done? Does Mother know?"

Alex and I both grimace and I answer. "May does know now."

Alex crosses his arms, agreeing with me. "I figured Mother would tell you soon enough. I wanted it kept secret until we were sure of our plans to leave here. And like I told you on the phone, we're going away together tomorrow and we won't come back. But in case no one told you this, I will. We—Jojo and I—we also have a daughter. You have a niece. She's almost six years old."

Grady leaps away from his desk, shouting, "A kid? A Wallace-Sinclair kid? No fucking way! No wonder! No wonder shit had to go so damn crazy! No wonder you're signing it all over to me without even a blink. Fuck! Alex." His eyes sweep wildly to me, processing. "Do you understand how dangerous it is, how it's a miracle the kid's lived to breathe in and out all of these years? Holy shit. You two—had a daughter. Forget the secret about the lake. Father...shit...he ...he..."

"He's dead, Grady," Alex says softly. "You don't have to think about what he would have thought or done. He didn't know and he's gone now. Please. You have to let him go." Alex lowers his voice and glances at me.

Grady's words have made my stomach hurt, because he's right. It is a miracle Mr. Sinclair never found out about Emily. After what I've heard today, it's a miracle she was even born, that they didn't kill me, too.

"Our daughter," Alex continues steadily. "She is why we are leaving. She is the reason I won't even flinch when I sign this deed over to you giving you the lake and the house. It's because she's got big brown eyes just like Mother's and because she's got our same fighting spirit. And it's because I trust that you must want this feud to end how I do. I trust that you won't come after us or hurt an innocent little girl who just might have a hint of a smile that looks like yours. Make me this promise. Be the end of this, Grady. Please. Let us go easily. You get to win—you win it all."

"It won't be me coming after you." Grady shakes his head and swallows, all of the fight going out of him so suddenly it surprises both of us. Grady's face is colorless, and his resigned sigh seeps out like a surrender. "I can make that promise to you. It won't ever be me."

"Thank you." Alex sits back, his face visibly relaxing.

I wipe away a new round of tears as I, too, become filled with relief at Grady's promise because it seemed so sincere. I suddenly understand how Alex went all the way to hell and back to protect me, because I'm doing it right now just to protect Emily.

Alex hands me a pen, and my vision is so blurred I can hardly write straight on the line Alex is pointing at on the deed.

A few minutes later, all documents have been signed and emailed to the attorneys by e-signatures. The only one with handwritten signatures is the old deed, which we scan and upload into digital format to be filed for the State of Washington's website and all of the Sinclair attorneys.

With the impossible seemingly behind us, Alex looks content. He's free. I bury any shreds of hatred or darkness I had left for Grady. I acknowledge they may never be gone completely, but my feelings about him are now covered with a vacuum of sheer relief as well as coated with such deep sadness about the abuse he and Alex had endured at the hands of their father.

As Alex tours Grady through the apartment, their banter becomes so natural and light that I can almost imagine Alex's dream of some sort of future relationship as true brothers becoming real one day.

In the bedroom, Grady opens Alex's closet with a

flourish, exclaiming over how nice it is inside the walk-in. And as they go through the things inside, Alex points out everything from how to use the safe to saying that his brother should try on his cashmere robe.

"Dude. I've never even worn it. Hell, never worn most of this stuff. It's new, and it's all yours. We're taking only what we can fit in our car."

"Nice that we're the same size, would be a shame to waste this stuff." Grady smirks as he slips the robe over his entire outfit. It's actually a little tight on him, but we go along with his fantasy.

As we return to the living room, Alex generously pours Grady a scotch on the rocks and shows him how to operate the integrated bar and entertainment center controls as well as the door locks and program that will let him change the entrance and elevator codes to lock us out whenever he's ready.

"I'm going to sleep over here tonight. Why the hell not. My new place," Grady announces, stretching his arms wide and looking around the dream bachelor pad.

Alex nods. "You should. It's late and the sheets are clean. The maids came today. Oh, which reminds me. Don't forget to pay them, because I'm going to be too broke to carry your cleaning services now."

Grady's grin falls off of his face as he realizes in that thick head of his just how much Alex has handed over to him.

"Dude. I can—I mean—if you need—"

"No." Alex cuts him off fast, but gently. "It's fine. We're all good. I don't want any of it. I don't need it."

Grady nods then flushes, perhaps feeling guilty about this for the very first time. I also wonder if we just witnessed Alex's brother growing tiny bits of an actual heart.

I avoid both of their gazes as Alex picks up my hand and pulls me to the elevator that will take us back down to our car.

"We'll be out of *your* lake house by tomorrow night. Whatever code you change this building too will also change the door codes over there. It's all integrated, and again anything that's left behind in that home is also yours to enjoy. And, Grady? Thank you. Thank you for letting me go like this. Truly. Thank you."

I lock eyes with him and nod my thanks, because tears have again flooded my throat, robbing me of speech.

As the elevator slides closed, Grady nods to us both, but he never says another word.

17.

ALEX, PRESENT DAY.

As I drove Jojo back to the lake, my heart felt lighter. I also felt happier. I was so free and all-powerful feeling that I thought I might suddenly be able to fly this SUV instead of just drive it out of here tomorrow. Jojo has been so quiet, typing into her phone off and on the entire way, that I haven't been able to tell if she is feeling happy, angry, or sad. But I don't press her because my guess is she's feeling all three. I know she's been remembering, and processing, just how I've been doing.

Finally, as we hit the crossroad that takes us to the fork that leads to our house one way or onto the overgrown road that would have taken us to my father's old hunting lodge, I slow the car and break into the silence. "Do we go get Emily and Shelly?"

"What? Oh, no. I'm sorry. I thought I'd said my thoughts out loud to you while I was texting them."

I shake my head, stopping the car. "You didn't."

"Shelly and Walt put Emily to bed, and they're settled in for the night. I told Aunt Shelly about the lake—and the deed. I asked her if it would be okay if you and I could say goodbye to the lake tonight...alone."

She sighs this weighted breath, so I take up her hand and give it a squeeze.

"I want to..." Her voice grows low and hoarse and at first I think it's tears about to flood in, but when she looks up at me, her gaze is so sweet and so heated my heart skips. "I want to swim with you one last time, and kiss warm cookies off your lips and body." She grins. "I want to make love to you out there on our rock." She laughs shyly before going on. "I want to say goodbye to it all—just you and me with the lake water on us, around us. What do you say?"

"Sounds perfect," I answer, letting her hand go. I'm already feeling blood rush into my cock as my foot hits the gas pedal, taking us straight up into the drive that leads to the lake house.

We start kissing before we're even through the garage door that leads us into the kitchen. I've got her shirt off by the dining area. She has my shirt off soon after, and I kick out of my shoes and pants somewhere in the middle of the living room. By the time we're heading out onto the deck, and onto the rock, she and I are naked, smiling and burning with need. We dive into the lake, the cool water slowing our desire as we splash and laugh with each other under the stars, pulling long strokes through the water but never drifting far apart.

Jojo turns, wading in the deep. She smirks at me just before she sets off fast, laughing because she knows I'm chasing her. When I catch her, I pull her in close, loving how my cock throbs heavy and ready against her bare ass. "Not so fast." I laugh with her, turning her slick, wet body to face me.

She gives up the fight and ducks in for a kiss while wrapping her arms around my neck and pressing her breasts—her tight, hard nipples—up into my chest. Her lips slant, half smiling and all desire as her tongue finds mine and mine hers. We both melt into each other. The kiss grows so deep we start to lose strength in our legs and our backs, and my cock is probing her, seeking entry into her even while we're standing in neck-deep water. She grabs it, ready to guide it the rest of the way. "Wait...no..."

"No?" She still has her hands on me. Her eyes are dark with desire as her palms squeeze all around me, those deft fingers of hers, teasing my tip, making me jerk. She licks her lips and grins.

"I'll come in two seconds if you aren't careful." I admonish her, peeling her hands off of me while I pause to lean down and take my revenge on her by sucking on one of those perfect tips. The feel of my mouth on her breast makes her shiver and gasp. I nearly lose it again as she leans her head so far back her hair dips into the water. She asks me in a sexy whisper to "do that to the other one."

When I'm finished with her request, she's limp, compliant and so hot I grow impatient. I scoop her up into my arms and walk with her back to the rock. "I want you on the rock, on your back with the stars reflecting down in your eyes. And I want to go slowly, and I want us both to nearly die in each other's arms here tonight...beginning with you."

"Oh...I love it when you begin with me..." She moves her lips up and captures mine in a biting, hungry kiss. When she's done, I lift her up and lay her back gently on the flattest, smoothest part of the rock, leaving her legs dangling off the sides, spread wide in front of me.

The sloping angle of the rock makes it easy for me to access all that I want, and while I'm looking up at her, I remember all of the times we did this here in the past. I smile and lick the inside of her thigh, bringing fingers close and rubbing her just how she likes it while my head and my tongue inch closer in, loving how she moans. She anticipates where I'm going to go next, squirming her hips up toward my mouth. Her hands bury in my hair and pull me lower between her legs.

"So bossy...so pushy..." I whisper my heat and touch my smile against her soft, pink skin. "Patience, love. Patience," I say before I begin working my tongue against her and into her.

She writhes against me, and pushes my head down harder with her hands. "I want to feel you come," I whisper against her, but she surprises me by pulling my head away.

"I…want…to feel *you*," she gasps out, biting her lips, her body bucking up, going totally against her words, and because she's so hot, I can't help but try to give her body what it wants. I shove two fingers into her—and then three. "Ahh—Alex," she moans. My cock jerks and throbs harder.

"I want more; I want you. *Fuck. Alex.*" She can't stop moving against me. "Fuck me. I want you inside of me. I want to feel you come. Please." She moves my hands away, opens her legs wide in front of me while she teases and pulls on her tits, eyes locked onto mine in heated melting want. "Please…"

It takes all of my strength to not slam into her, but I know I can't. Though I think she wouldn't mind it, the rock under her and how I want to pound into her would hurt her. I won't mar her beautiful body. Quickly, I bend and scoop her up into my arms and bring her inside into the living room couch. I lay her on it and in seconds I'm inside of her, slamming her back into the cushions, loving how she gasps and takes me deep inside. She squeezes me so soft and so hard all at the same time. She moans and cries out my name, and I fall into a trance at the way her breasts move back and forth, those hard, pink tips straining toward my mouth. She meets every thrust until we both come so hard I swear I've either broken the couch or there's been an earthquake under us.

Or both.

We sleep for an hour naked and alone, crumpled into each other until I wake up to find her pushing her body into me again. I moan happily as she's skillfully managed to slip me into her from the back, arching her ass up and against me until I'm wide awake and fucking her all over again.

"Hold up," I say, needing more room to do everything I want to do. "As hot as this is," I whisper out, "there's no way you can be comfortable like this."

Keeping my cock deep inside of her, I manage to stand and flip her up on her knees. She takes temporary control and pulls her pulsing heat away from me, leaving me on my knees in the center of the couch, my cock cold and desolate without her. "How about this way?" she asks, one upping my idea as she walks around to the backside of the couch, quirking up a brow and licking her lips as she lays her self over the tall back of the sofa. My gaze goes over her flushed cheek turned to the side, her tangled mass of hair, and the way her breasts are pressing into the cushions.

"Fuck yes," I say, not really even sure how I've moved from where I was to standing behind her, about to come all over her ass because the sight of her waiting for me like this is nearly impossible to hold on through. Trying to get some calm back into my body, I run my hands along the line of her spine and slide them around to the front of where she's pressed herself against the leather back of the couch. I rub her there—slowly and gently—

listening to her moan and whisper *yes* over and over again against a pillow. I let my cock just rest against the back of her folds. I tease us both with almost-touches.

I've nearly got control, but then she looks back over her shoulder, in the middle of her moans and her own pleasure, and somehow tilts that ass up and gets her clit to pull in my tip just one fraction more than I wanted it to go. Suddenly, I've got my hands on her hips, and I'm pushing into her.

She calls out my name when we come this time, and it's so deep and so hard and so endless that I wonder if, in nine months, Emily's going to have a sibling. Then I hope and pray that it could be so, that the lake could give us one last gift.

When her moans stop, she's limp and smiling shyly at me. "Wow...I'm sorry if I was a bit too demanding and—"

I pull her close to me and kiss away her next words. "Never, ever apologize for sex like *that*. Thank you."

She laughs, cuddling into my chest. "Thank you back, then. I want to do it again." She laughs. "Tomorrow though; I need sleep."

I scoop her up and head with her into the master bedroom then carry her to our bed.

When we're all snuggled into the covers and I'm holding her in my arms, she asks softly, "Are you sad to leave here? Any regrets at all?"

"I can't wait, Jojo. I've never been happier in my life."

AFTER SHE FALLS ASLEEP, I find that I can't. So I decide I'll pack up the few things that can't be left behind, which, I realize, does not comprise very many things. I head to my office and pull out all of my personal files, things like my passport, all of my *non-Sinclair*-related investments that did not get signed over to Grady last night, and I shove them into an empty Rubbermaid tub I find in the closet. While I work, I replay the conversation we had with Grady in my head.

I hope he's happy. I hope he feels the sincerity of what we signed last night. And if he's not happy now, I do hope one day he truly will be.

As the dawn light starts creeping in, I walk the half-filled bucket directly out to the Tahoe. When I make my way back to the living room, I pause to fix the couch, moving it the few feet it needs to go so it's back into its usual position after we'd knocked it halfway around the room last night. I also pick up the pillows we scattered around, then pause to pick up our discarded clothes that litter all of the rooms like giant confetti.

Smiling now, and half turned on as I scoop Jojo's lacy bra off the floor, I retrace our steps all the way to the kitchen where our shoes, her panties, and my pants and boxers still lie. When I reach the back door, my eyes land on our ancient fishing rods. It looks like we knocked them sideways as we rushed in. As I right them, I smile more. Jojo has been wearing the engraved lure I made for her since the day she and I reunited. Since the funeral.

I almost forgot the rods she shoved in that rental car when I returned it the day after Grady attacked her, but the lot attendant found them when he popped the trunk. These rods gave me and Jojo so much happiness. And that lure was my awkward high school way of telling Jojo how much I loved her when I couldn't say the words myself. The fact that she'd worn it on her heart— and acts like she will wear it forever now—means more to me than anything I could ever own, and when we leave here, we will take those rods with us and leave them in sight wherever we go.

Satisfied with that thought, I return to the kitchen where I left my messenger bag last night, and pull out my copies of the documents as well as the newly signed deed to the lake and the aquifer because I have this urge to touch them. I just want to make sure I didn't dream it all.

I read over every word of it as I make a huge pot of coffee, but when I get to the last paragraph my heart nearly stops beating.

The document states that the lake—the lake doesn't belong to me, or to Grady, or to Jojo at all! It wasn't mine to give. Not now.

My stomach flips with nausea as I read on. As I read it again.

"Fuck..." I mutter out, grabbing a pen and under-lining the words *descendant* and *offspring*. As I read, I underline that word five more times, because… "Fuck!" I say again. According to this newly signed document, the lake—the aquifer—everything I once owned here now belongs to our offspring. To *Emily*.

It was buried in the finest of print, along with that document Jojo found of her mother's agreement with my father. They were words we all took for granted last night. Words left from the original. The document states that should there be any *offspring* to the Sinclair heirs, that the lake and the aquifer will go immediately to said offspring.

While I named Grady as the head of the family in the paperwork last night, Emily was *alive* when I was officially the head. She was alive when I married her mother and made it all legal this week, which means that in a court of law, the deed belongs to her! Worse, it will belong to her, with the Sinclair *head of family* to hold guardianship over until she's twenty-one years old!

My stomach churns again as I let the ramifications of that sink in. If this document is allowed to stay like this, Grady will have huge talons sunk into Emily's life, year after year. It's a Sinclair life sentence.

I know I need to get in my car and drive back to my —to Grady's penthouse. I need to face him with this, and convince him to change the wording with me. I need to tell him I didn't know…that I want to work with our lawyers or, hell, at this point I'm willing to lie and forge something that makes it all his now. I need to come clean to him about this knowledge before he wakes up, too, because he's going to think I've betrayed him. He's going to assume that I knew it all along and that I was trying to trick him...just how Father would have.

He'll think I was going to drive away with my daughter being the sole owner of the lands and properties he wanted the most, leaving him powerless to do anything with them at all.

I slide on some flip-flops, pull on my shirt from last night, and pen a quick note to Jojo so she won't worry if she wakes up early. Placing it near her on the bed, I grab my car keys and wallet off my side table, smiling at her as she sighs and turns over in her sleep.

I will forge Jojo's signature again if needed. She won't care. She trusts me completely. My brother also won't care as long as it looks legal and he believes we mean, once again, to end all claims on the land as promised. As I rush out toward the garage, I grab the original deed and my entire messenger bag and head to my car.

If Jojo sees one word of what's written on this deed it will scare her more than it's scared me. She could think I've betrayed her too. She would never believe we're free from my family. Worse, she'll never think Emily is truly safe, maybe not even from me, because after all—I am still a Sinclair.

I vow to have it all corrected, rewritten and re-signed by the time she wakes up. At least by the time we drive the hell out of this place forever.

18.

ALEX, PRESENT DAY.

My phone starts buzzing and the caller ID says GRADY.

"Damn," I grumble. He's probably awake reading the same shit I'm reading right now and royally pissed off. He's going to think I've tricked him.

I push to accept his call from my dash, and I start talking fast before he can utter a word. "Grady. I was going to call you. I just woke up and reread the deed. The lake belongs to our daughter. To *Emily*. We need to fix that."

"You hid her from me. From all of us. Father always said I'm stupid, and I guess I am..."

"You're not stupid. We're both stupid. It was a mistake..."

"He said that, too. Mistakes. That's what you and me are to him. He said we're too much like our mother. Weak. Stupid. He's finished with us."

His words are all twisted; the pressure of this—of our lives--has finally taken his mind. He's also distraught, like he can't breathe...or maybe...like he's... crying? No. Impossible. Not Grady. Not in front of me. Never where I can hear it.

"Dude. It's fine. We simply didn't read the small print."

"Father told us to always read the small print," he grunts out.

I think it's sad that he still seeks Father's approval, even when the man is dead. "I'm on my way with the laptop, the original deed, everything. We'll rewrite it all. We can fix it."

"You think you're so smart—keeping that kid a secret. All these years, I thought Father was proud of me. Even proud of you sometimes...shit..." He coughs— and then coughs again, nearly a choke. I wonder, and then worry—*is he wheezing?* He sounds like he can't get air.

"I didn't know about her either, Grady. I didn't know..." I say, trying to keep the conversation going. When he doesn't answer, just wheezes into the phone, I ask, "Dude. Are you okay?"

"You didn't even tell me her name last night—you sneaky mother-fucking *liar*! And I fell for it! I should have known her name, don't you think? *Emily*. A niece. A Sinclair granddaughter. Now, she'll be the heir to replace us both."

Grady laughs like a man about to dive from a

rooftop, driven to a psychotic break from grief and abuse. I try to process what's going on with his coughing, too. It sort of sounds like he's so upset he's having an asthma attack. Only, Grady doesn't have asthma. Maybe he's drunk? That's more like him, and when we left him last night he was well into the glass of scotch I poured for him, so maybe he finished the whole bottle, staying up all night on a binge.

"Yes. Emily. That is her name." As I drive into the outskirts of Tacoma, I work to calm him with honest answers. "Please be clear that I'm not hiding anything."

Like I'd done last night, I try to make Grady see Emily as a real person instead of someone he should hate. "She's tiny. A ball of sheer joy. She's good and sweet and has hair exactly like Jojo's."

"And a smile—a little like mine, you said," he whispers.

"Yes! She's also got a fighter's spirit that's like yours. When she falls down and scrapes a knee or an elbow she never cries. She just tells me that she's okay."

"It's the Sinclair way." He sighs out, continuing, "So she's small?"

"She's going into kindergarten. Do you remember being in kindergarten?"

"Yes. It was the first year Father beat the hell out of me—that I can remember anyhow. He said I was a big boy now and needed to be able to handle the pain. You don't remember. You were in diapers."

"Pain for pain," I whisper, remembering how I also

got a beating in kindergarten. How I missed two weeks of school and how Mother wasn't allowed to tuck me in or even see me until I could get myself out of bed.

He coughs again then breathes heavily into the phone. "I always believed Father when he said you were the one that always fell for his games. That you were notorious and consistent for being played. He said you were like some sitting duck, buying into the tricks we played on you. *You're* supposed to be the easy mark—not me. Never me. I thought I had greater value, you know?" He coughs again. "But I guess—*fuck*. Alex…" Another cough. "Joke's on me."

He wheezes, then adds, "Tell me, Alex. How are you going to fix this? How are you going to try and rush in and save everyone this time? Despite everything, will you still save me too?"

"Yes," I answer automatically, mind rushing in a million directions now. "If you need saving I will try."

He laughs. "Of course I won't put that on you. I get now that I don't deserve any kind of saving. None."

"What?" Confused, I shake my head, trying to process his words, trying to calm his thoughts that I've betrayed him. "Please believe me. It's an easy fix to add an addendum to this deed. I'll make it read however you want. I'll call the lawyers right now. I don't want you to be so upset. My words, my feelings about us last night, were sincere."

"I want you to know I believe that."

"I'm almost there—I was already in the car driving to you to make this right when you called."

"Too late. Don't come…"

"Grady…" I floor it, the front of the SUV lifting with the speed. "Five minute or less and this will be solved."

"You left them alone? Tiny, small Emily? And…Jojo? They're alone?" He sounds incredulous. "Again. See? So stupid. Why, Alex? Or did you bring them with you? Are they in the car?"

Because he sounds slightly hysterical, and because I'm used to a lifetime of not trusting him, my gut wrenches at his line of questioning. Stomach sinking with doubts about leaving Jojo behind, I deliberately don't answer him. Instead I try to divert him by blabbing about the topic of the deed.

"If we can't get her out of the deed, we will draw up a letter that makes you the executor. And—and—we'll both sign it and refile with the state. Should something happen to you, those rights can revert back to the Sinclair head of family. Which will become me—though that is the last thing I want." I remind him of my own goals, to cut ties with the Sinclair family forever. "When Emily's twenty-one, I promise you, I'll promise it every damn year in blood until it happens, that she will sign away her rights to the land and to the lake and to the aquifer or whatever is left of it. It's my solemn oath to you."

"Blood," Grady whispers. "Poor little Emily." His voice fades like he's walked away from his phone. He begins shouting from a distance. "I fucking fell for it—just like you always did. You were right last night. I am tired of the feud. I'm satisfied it's going to end this way. Happy that I'm going to be done."

His voice grows more muffled, and his slurring grows worse.

"Nothing has changed, Grady. Nothing has changed," I shout, barreling my car through the downtown area, hoping he's not so drunk that he's just passed out. I try to keep him lucid and awake, shouting into the phone, "Grady! One signature, and we're done. One document, and we're both going to be done. This car is already half-packed as promised, and you'll never see any of us again after today. Never. Not unless you *want* to see your family."

"My family...ha! It's a terrible painful thing, *my family*." He's moved back closer to his phone, but he's still not holding it to him.

"You're right about one thing though." He laughs darkly. "Nothing's changed, Alex. It's all *so* fucked up. You. Me. Betrayal. Family. *Fucking Sinclairs!*"

He sighs out long and loud, voice trembling. "I'm so tired, Alex. Aren't you tired? And...fuck, it's so late for this, but I'm sorry. I'm really sorry for everything I did. People who believe..." He gasps out like he's choking again. "*Those people.* They say you can ask for forgiveness and shit at the end. They say if you're truly sorry maybe you won't burn in hell, and I'm so tired of hell, Alex. I don't want to go there again. I hope you'll tell Jojo.

When she forgave me last night…that felt good. I know I don't deserve it, but I believed her."

As I park across the street from the building, I transfer the call from my car console into my phone so I can run through the street, keeping him on the line as I look up to the penthouse windows above and find all of the lights have been turned on.

My brother is standing there, silhouetted like he's leaning against the glass. My gut sinks with instant terror. *Don't jump.*

"I see you. You're good. I'm not." He's sobbing.

"I see you, too. And we're not different, Grady," I answer quietly, looking up at him. My breath starts coming out hard, as if I've run the entire distance from the lake to this place. "Please let me up; you're sort of scaring me. Let me up. Let me fix this. Please."

"I won't. I've changed all the access codes, so don't even try; just stay there. Stay there for a minute so I can see you down there. So I don't feel so alone." He places his arms wide against the glass and lays his hands flat, his body making the shape of a cross. With all of the light streaming out from behind him, he looks like he's trying to fly.

"You're not alone, Grady," I whisper, holding still and staring up at him. "Please let me up." My heart is squeezing, and my guts are filling up with an ocean of dread as he falls to his knees like he's got no strength left in his legs. He sobs more.

"What the fuck is wrong, Grady? What?" I stare up at

his figure in the window. I've never, ever heard my him cry like this before. "What are the new codes to the building?"

"Six. Seven. Five. Three. You'll need them for the lake house. Father only has the old ones. He will be angry about that."

"Father?" I'm now certain Grady has lost his hold on reality.

"Father. Yes. He's known about Emily all along. He faked his own fucking death to lure Jojo back here. He's waited all of these weeks—he's been waiting for Emily to be his. We didn't know about her, Mother and I. He made Mother plan his funeral. Even I didn't know because he told me I'd have fucked it up. He also made her go and meet Jojo, so they could lure Emily in. He said it would be perfect for the child to have herNana there when she finds out both of her parents are dead."

My heart slows. My skin turns cold, and all I can whisper into the phone is *"Father..."*

"I'm supposed to lure you up here somehow. But you —your fucking endless guilt and honesty has made it too easy. You were already on the way. Father wants me to kill you, Alex. And then, even though he's just broken...like...five of my bones, he expects me to meet him at the lake to help with Jojo. He told me I can have her, but he's lying. He would never allow that. He just wants to kill her."

"Where is Father?" I ask, keeping my voice calm and

deliberate. I need information. I need it now. "Where is Father now?"

"He's been hiding in his hunting lodge this whole time. Until last night. Until you sent the little girl into the wolf's den and scared him out."

My stomach drops, and I nearly vomit. "Don't feel bad about falling for it, Alex. Until Father walked in and beat the shit out of me last night, I thought he was truly dead, too. He waited for the scotch to zap my strength. He'd been watching. Ha...motherfucker is always watching, isn't he?"

I duck low next to my car, glancing wildly around me, wondering if this is some sort of trap, if there's going to be a gunman, or hell, even a cop that's supposed to come out here and shoot the shit out of me right now under some false, bribe-infested pretense my father drummed up.

"Don't worry. You're safe out there. I can read your mind...even from way up here. Always could; your poker face still sucks ass." Grady laughs a little, but it's a sad, pained sound. "Father left explosives, big ones, that I'm supposed to use to destroy this place once I knock you out up here. Everyone else in here—the doorman, and the people in the businesses below—were supposed to be casualties. News distraction. But I know how to get them out. I won't do any of it. I'm ready to stand up to Father. Ready to be an uncle. A good uncle."

The building's fire alarm starts shrieking, and the security guard as well as the doorman who's reporting to work along with a couple of maids come out into the street.

"Please, Alex! Go back now," Grady whispers. "Find your family. Sneak in through the woods. Father just left here. He said he was going to start at the hunting lodge. He thinks it's going to be easy. Mother's been waiting for him in the little boathouse all night as ordered. He won't be expecting you to be alive. He's waiting for Jojo to show up there. He'll be waiting for me and Mother, too."

My brother's voice still crackles from the phone but it sounds so very far away. My mind screams, telling my legs to move back into my car, mentally already working to make some sort of plan.

"Forgive yourself, Alex. We couldn't have known. I'm with you now. I should have been with you all along."

Sirens fill the air as I re-enter my car and slam the door shut. As I'm pulling away, a boom erupts that's so huge the entire street under my car shakes. Glass, metal, and burning bits of fiery debris rain down on top my car and all around me. Ears ringing, and heart thundering with panic-adrenaline, I glance up, searching for Grady again, but I know he's gone. More than gone.

The entire top half of the building is missing.

He saved me. But for what? If everything else Grady said is true, he's saved me just in time to go back to my lake and find my sweet Jojo dead, my little girl hurt or worse, and under my Father's fucked-up control.

"*Fuck!*" I shout, slamming my steering wheel with my

fists, horrified that my brother just died right in front of me. Even more horrified by the thought that maybe Grady's last move was not one of kindness at all. Maybe it was his last revenge. His way to end me slowly, because right now, maybe my brother has finally beat me. Being already dead seems the better place to be if Father's still alive.

That thought forces me to clear my head. It makes me remember his last words. Grady didn't beat me. He saved me. His voice ricochets in my head.

I'm with you now.

"Stay with me, Grady. Help me. God. Please. Please. Please." I wipe tears off my face, but instead of speeding directly back to the lake house how I want to, I get my shit together enough to quickly circle around the burning building and pull my car around the side of it while I pull in my breath and force myself to think while I dial Jojo.

"Think, Alex. Think. If Father's alive, what is he doing? Who is he watching? *Think*," I order myself. My finger shakes and cramps just as I'm about to push CALL to tell Jojo what's happening. Instead, I delete her number and nearly vomit all over again because I know I nearly almost ruined my advantage.

"Fuck!" I cry out again. I delete Jojo's cell number and roll down my window to toss out my phone deep into the bushes at the base of the burning building. Of course Father's tracking me; it's something he's always done. He's probably been listening to each and every phone call and reading each text Jojo and I have shared. And he's probably paid someone to hack into any and every text Jojo shares with her aunt, too.

I can't risk texting or calling Jojo to warn her, because that would warn my father, too. Even though it hurts and it may kill Jojo, anyone involved in this latest fucked up Michael Sinclair plan needs to think I'm dead.

Just as the first police and firetruck sirens scream into the front of the building, I make a break away from my car, tucking my messenger bag under my arm and running full-tilt toward the car rental place nearby as though the devil himself is chasing me.

Because that's what my father is. The Devil.

Only, this time, unlike all of the others, I am ready to die. I'm ready to take everyone and anyone I love with me before letting him win.

19.

JOJO, PRESENT DAY.

I wake in a jolt, suddenly not sure where I am. For a flash of a moment, everything around me is unfamiliar, but it sinks in soon.

I'm home. Home for now.

It's my last day at the only *real* home that's ever been just Alex's and mine. I'm going to miss this lake terribly, but I can't tell Alex that because it would crush him.

As much as I love this place that Alex built just for me, it's enough having been able to spend these few days in it. It will always be a part of my best memories, and I adore Alex for giving our reunion such a perfect backdrop.

Stretching my arms out above my head, I let the soft sheets fall from my body as I sit up and turn to find the bed empty next to me. There's a note on the pillow with a small peppermint resting on top to weigh it down. I unwrap the candy and pull the page to my lap to read.

Good morning, Mrs. Wallace-Sinclair! Pack up anything you think you need, and gather all of Emily's things to get ready to load. I'm out for a little adventure, but I'll be back soon!

;-)

Alex

My mouth curls at his choice of words—*out for a little adventure.* I came here to bring him back from the brink and I did. He was never going to have adventures again, but all of that has changed now. From here forward, life is nothing but adventures for the three of us.

I'm sure he's gone fishing, and I'm a little jealous. I would have woken up with the sun to join him. I was always a better fisherman anyhow, despite what I let him think. Before I let myself feel too bad though, I think about how this is also Alex's chance to say goodbye to this place. He deserves his own time with the water and the trees.

I slip into my comfortable joggers and one of Alex's shirts, and put on my best running shoes, wanting something comfortable for the long drive ahead. I twist my hair on top of my head and set off to work, taking care of the few things of mine in the bedroom drawers and closet, then wandering the other rooms of the house in search of things I'm sure we'll need. There isn't much, and honestly, some of the things I've collected we can easily live without. A few electronics like the Kindle and the portable speaker make it into a duffle bag along with chargers for our phones, medicines, bandages and alcohol pads. It's a modern first-aid kit, but besides that and our clothes, there's nothing else we really need. We have each other.

On my final lap, my eyes land on our old fishing rods, and though I know it's silly and too sentimental because he's got way better gear now, I feel slightly sad that he didn't take the original rods that started it all between us on his last fishing trip to his lake.

Our lake...

I send Alex a text to see where he is and ask when he's coming back. Smiling, I also tell him I love him. Then, I fire one off to Aunt Shelly: *Is everyone awake over there?*

Walking back into the bedroom, I sit down on the edge of the bed, staring at the duffle bags and suitcases that are full of my and Emily's few belongings, along with whatever else I think might be useful to us on this road trip. It's all packed and ready to go at my feet.

The phone is still balanced in my palm, but neither Alex or my aunt have responded yet. I will it—pray for it to buzz with a message from either of them.

Shelly writes back first.

All is well. Me and Walt are up, and we just got Emily moving. See you very soon.

I send back a quick *okay*, and still waiting for Alex's response, I bring the phone into the bathroom with me, balancing it on the counter so I can see it light up while I shower, just in case I don't hear it ding.

I end up staring at it through the glass shower the

entire time, rushing through a quick shampoo and rinse. I stare while I towel off and slip back into my travel clothes. Even though I know it's impossible to text when you're fly-fishing, which is probably what he's doing, I send Alex one more message.

Love? Can you at least tell me where you've gone? North side? South side? Catch anything? Text me an update if you get a chance. I'm nearly all packed. Feeling lonely...

My eyes catch on the hallway closet, and I decide to add some of Alex's heavy coats to our pile of things. We haven't discussed exactly where we're going to settle yet, but I would like to try going back to Ohio. Jeff hasn't terminated the lease on our apartment, so I'll have to deal with that and all of the belongings Emily and I left behind anyhow. And maybe Alex will like it there. It's as good a place as anywhere. There's something quaint about Waterton, the small town that sheltered me for nearly six years. It snows there, blanketing the cottages with white pillows that turn the nearly century-old village into a Hallmark card every winter. The schools are great, staffed with teachers who have been in their same jobs for years, and Emily has friends there. The one thing I've missed out here is seeing my daughter laugh on the swings at the park with other kids her age. Wherever we land, it will be good to get our daughter back into a real routine.

As I load the jackets into transportable piles, I distract myself from this uneasy feeling that is settling in my gut by forcing myself to think about what's next for us.

Maybe I can waitress again to keep the bills paid for a time, and Alex...he'll be able to do anything. This clean slate will let him decide exactly the man he wants to be. No more business deals and land brokering, unless that's what he wants. I have a feeling he won't, though. I think his heart and mind are destined for greater things.

After nearly thirty more minutes have gone by, my worry starts to boil over, and still no texts have come in from Alex. I tell myself that it's because he has hiked or maybe even canoed to the far side of the lake. There's some rock outcroppings there, ones that kill all cell signal when you're standing under them. Which is where he will be standing—if he is, in fact, fishing his favorite deep pools one last time.

I carry my phone with me outside and walk off the deck and onto the edge of our flat rock. I note there's an odd haze in the sky, pollution from Seattle maybe? I don't ponder over that much because I'm glancing down both shorelines, searching for Alex's lone figure, or at least hoping to see ripples in the water or flashes of movement from where he may be casting or hiking back, but I see nothing.

Nothing at all.

"*Alex!*" His name comes back to me, echoing *Alex...Alex.*

I yell one more time, "Alex?"

Alex...Alex.

I hold my breath, watching a few fish leap and splash near me while I listen closely for his voice coming over the wind, or coming from the trail in the trees.

Still nothing.

I look at my phone and dial him directly this time, letting it ring and ring until it goes to voicemail, before repeating the call again. I call him five times. All end the same way. My gut is twisting so much now I have trouble breathing, and because I know I'm being silly, I send another text to Shelly, asking if she wants me to drive over and grab them, or if they prefer to walk home down the path?

It's a lovely day, darling. Not far at all. We'll walk to you, give you more time to pack.

I stare at her words, and wonder why her response has unnerved me even more, because suddenly I have this thought—that something is not right. Not right at all.

I respond quickly. *I've packed all that I can pack.*

I hit send and wait for her reply, watching as the typing dots wave at me for several long seconds.

Nonsense. There must be something you've missed. Take your time and check again.

My brow pulls in, that nagging worry now has every whistle alarming in my head about these texts. Something is really off. I respond again. *I'm going to load our bags in the car, then I'll hike out and meet you halfway. Cool?*

I wait for a beat for her response, but she doesn't reply right away this time. I put my phone in my back pocket and gather up the bags and the jackets and head toward the garage. I stop at the door when I feel my pocket buzz.

We shall need a little more time to get Emily situated with breakfast. But tell me when you're on the way so we can watch for you, would you?

I answer. *Yes. Sure, and thanks again Aunt Shelly.*

She sounds different. Maybe she's just cranky or tired. She could also be doing one of those talk-to-texts things while distracted trying to get Emily fed and ready to go. Emily can sometimes act like six cats all going in different directions.

Even though I know it's irrational and very impatient of me, I dial Alex one more time, but just like every time before, it goes to voicemail. The lure pin is sitting on the counter where I left it the night before, so I walk inside and grab it to tuck into my purse but pause before I put it away completely. I pull my hand back out to squeeze it tightly. I think I'll hold it awhile. I think I *need* to.

"Damn, Alex. Where are you?"

I DECIDE to brew myself a mug of coffee for the car ride, but before I flip it on, I catch the still-warm full cup Alex must have left for me. How long has this been here? I turn on the kitchen flat screen to get a handle on any weather we'll be facing on our way out of town then pour my cup. After a sip, I head back to the bags in the bedroom and drag them all to the back garage door entry. Pulling it open, I hold the door there with my foot while I reach inside to feel for the light switch for the garage.

My heart skips a beat. Alex's car is gone—the garage is empty!

It takes me two full seconds to understand what I'm seeing and work out how that fits with the scenario I had in my head. Alex hasn't gone fishing. He's driven somewhere.

I let the door go, but as it pulls back in, it drags a paper along with it that had been caught on the floor. I bend down and pick it up with my free hand, recognizing the crumpled deed we'd signed yesterday almost instantly.

Dialing Alex again, both hands quivering, I take the deed back inside, leaving everything else stacked by the door. I flatten the pages on the kitchen counter and begin to scan.

The word *offspring* has been underlined on the deed numerous times.

"Offspring..." I mutter, thinking that it's referring to Grady and Alex, the offspring of Michael Sinclair, but then my eyes widen, shocked as I remember how my mom had also written about offspring and descendants in her sad and horrible letter that I found after the funeral. Only, as this reads, I realize the word *offspring* applies to *Emily*! We've all signed this and locked it into place—Emily's fate!

Alex would have made sure her future was protected and sheltered from any of the feud bullshit, wouldn't he? Or...God." I gulp, reading every single word for myself as my heart drops through the floor. Instantly, I begin to drown in doubts and fears about the Sinclair family like a face punch. Alex told me last night that all of this was a done deal. He said it over and over again, but according to this, it's not over.

Emily is now the owner of the land, the aquifer, and the oil. And Grady's signature cements this in place even more!

"Why? Why didn't I read the document myself last night?" I choke out, hardly able to breathe as I grow angry over my own stupidity.

Why did I trust Alex? How easily I've let down my guard and fallen into old patterns. I've been so careless. I let him meet Emily. And he's gone—not responding—and my daughter is not here with me. Are they together? Is all of this another Sinclair set up?

I'm spiraling. Desperate to figure out where Alex is *exactly*, I open the Find My iPhone App, and plug in Alex's email as well as the passwords he's given me to get on the internet here at the house, hoping they will match.

I'm in quickly—it's working. My heart actually stops beating when I see the location of Alex's phone.

He's back at the penthouse.

He's with Grady.

How long has he been there? Did he fuck me, lie to me, and leave laughing the moment I fell asleep? Did he leave to meet up with Grady and gloat over how easy I was to get this time?

"No. No. *No!*" I cry out, pushing my phone away along the counter and hating the thoughts firing through my head. This game, his father's game—it's poisoned me against faith.

Believe in him, I remind myself. Alex is good. Maybe he saw what I saw on the deed and he went to fix everything, only he accidentally dropped the deed as he drove away. Yes. That's more like him.

My stomach heaves with more nausea as fear for Emily and my doubts rush in harder. Alex convinced me to marry him so quickly—and maybe he was lying the whole time. Just like back in high school. Maybe, after he found out about Emily, he had to make sure he could show the world that Emily was also legally his so he— the Sinclair's—could keep their holdings.

So they could keep her!

I squeeze my eyes shut tightly at that last thought. My mind is betraying me, falling into a dangerous habit that comes along with the name Sinclair.

I refuse to believe this—that's not who Alex is.

As if the universe wanted me to snap out of my thoughts, the coffee machine buzzes just as the kitchen television screen shows the scene of a familiar building. It's the penthouse building, and people are running in every direction, and there's...smoke? In the background of the reporter's shot, I see Alex's car, and my heart flattens.

I turn the volume up just in time to hear the reporter say, "The entire top two floors of the building are gone. More like obliterated. From where I'm standing, John, it looks like a complete loss here at the Sinclair's premiere office and luxury lofts property. The entire street has been blocked off, and until all gas lines in the area can be checked, a five-mile radius has been evacuated as a precautionary measure. No one is yet certain as to what's caused this major explosion."

My eyes lock onto the shot and what looks like a half-ton of debris covering Alex's black Tahoe—*the car we're supposed to drive away in today.*

I whimper, losing my breath in bursts. "No, no, no, no...this is not real..." The words blubber from my lips.

I flip stations feverishly, hoping to see conflicting news somewhere else. I'm going mad, the camera shots are always the same, the building blown to bits in every frame. Alex's car always parked right where it shouldn't be.

I flip back to the first station in time to hear something that begins hopeful. "Hold on. Hold on. I'm getting some more breaking news."

I grip the counter's edge so hard that several of my nails bend and snap along the surface.

"In addition to this explosion that has shut down the entire Tacoma Downtown area, we have just received reports that a forest fire has broken out near the lodge that was once owned by the direct descendant of our town's founding father, Michael Sinclair. As most of you know, it's the largest stretch of undeveloped property in the Pacific Northwest, thousands of acres of woods and open space, leading all the way to the sound. And that property is owned by the same person who also owns this destroyed building behind me."

The man smiles like this is good news, not bad, before continuing. "Reports say the fire is located at the remotest edge of Sinclair Lake, I've been told, and the entire area seems to be under threat of being ravaged by it. High winds are not cooperating. We haven't been able to reach Alex Sinclair or his brother, Grady Sinclair, for comment yet, but several authorities are racing to the fire scene now. We also have our chopper on the way to help determine the scope of this second fire. We'll bring you more on that when it's available."

My stomach roils, and I rush to the sink, vomiting up disbelief, acid and sheer terror.

Because I feel like I'm about to pass out, I flip the faucet on high and scoop water into my mouth, spitting it out over and over again while I reach with my hand to turn up the volume in case I hear him say that he was wrong, but instead the footage flips back into the indoor news team and a woman, who's shaking her head in fake concern. "As you all may remember, Michael Sinclair was loved by nearly all of Tacoma, and less than two months ago, he was found dead of a gunshot wound to his head. It's hard not to think that with this suspicious downtown explosion plus the fire located on Sinclair lands?" She arches her brow in a well-practiced look at the camera. "There is speculation that this company—or this family—is possibly somehow under attack."

The dark-haired man on the news team answers her. "Authorities haven't said it for certain yet, Candace, but it does smell like foul play. We have been told to inform everyone living, hiking or camping in the wooded area to please evacuate as quickly as possible. The severe dry conditions plus today's winds have already made the size of this fire spread to six hundred acres."

Those words stick in my head hard. *Foul play. Foul play...but who's playing the game? Is it Alex? Is it Grady? Did May blow up her own two sons in that penthouse—and—my God! There's a fire—I have to get to Emily! I have to get us out of here.*

My knees wobble but I head directly toward Alex's office as I dial Shelly fast. Of course she doesn't pick up, so I leave a message.

"Shelly. You and Walt need to head down the path." A choked sob escapes as I say what I'm sure they're already running from. "There's a fire. *Please call me if you can. I need to know you're okay. Hurry!*"

I stop to grab the loaded pistol Alex keeps in his office closet and shove it in my pocket, and as I'm running out the door, I start coming up with new reasons for why no one has answered me.

They're all dead. That's the harshest thought. At the

top of the pathway where the forest grows thick and the trail leading to the lodge goes into a single track, I'm horrified that I haven't connected with anyone on the path, but my phone finally buzzes and rings in my hand.

I'm so startled that I nearly drop it. When I connect I hear Emily's sweet little voice on the other end. "Mommy? There's a fire. A big fire. Are you coming?"

I pull in a full breath. She's alive—she's scared, but she's alive. It takes everything I have to sound normal, which I'm sure I don't at all. I feel the vibrations in my words. "Baby. I'm coming. Where are you love? Are you on the trail heading back to the house?"

"No. The fire got too big. We went the other way. To the lake. I want you to come though. Ajax ran away. I'm so scared." Her voice sounds tremulous, like she's about to cry but being very brave.

"I'm coming. I am," I say. "Just tell me where you are." I start jogging again up the trail and in the direction of the smoke, because it's all I can do. "Can I speak to Aunt Shelly or Walt?"

"You can't. Aunt Shelly's not here. She and uncle Walt got locked in, and they told me I had to go. They told me I had to be very sneaky and fast. Aunt Shelly put her phone into my pocket. I'm calling because we're finally safe now."

I stop running again and start to tremble uncontrollably, taking all of my strength to keep myself from screaming at her. "What do you mean *we*, sweetie? Are you with...Daddy?"

"We ran to a boat. To the lake where there is water because water puts out fires. That's the safest place to go, right?"

"You're right baby. That's very good thinking." As I pick up my steady pace, the air around me begins to swirl with thick smoke, and though I can't see any flames, I can feel a shift in the air—the heat of it—the way it's swirling and making me cough. I sense the actual fire must be close now.

"Who are you *with*, Emily?" I ask firmly. "I need to speak to an adult."

"I'm with Nana, but she can't talk. She's sleeping. She said we had to run and hide, and the running made her very dizzy. Grandfather was there, and he's not nice like Nana is nice."

"Grandfather...?" I stumble and sink to my knees, staring at the ever-blackening sky as cracks in my chest break open wide.

Grandfather!

As I see flames cresting trees a quarter of a mile ahead of me, I'm broken wide open at this information. I wonder if I'm dead and in hell. But it's worse than that. I'm alive and I'm in hell.

As huge chunks of ash rain down around me, all of the puzzle pieces fall into place.

Michael Sinclair is alive. He's faked his death, and now has blown up his own sons because of the feud. Because of greed. Because he always wins.

Only...it's more than that. I'm certain now that Alex

and Grady are dead. Blown up so big that no one will ever find one shred of them left. No evidence or a trace that any of it existed at all.

Erased.

From the sounds of what Emily's just said, May must have been beaten and could be near death too. Walt, and my Aunt Shelly, are burning up in the fire that's so huge that no one will ever find their bodies either. Which means, if this is all true, I'm going to die next. Because this whole time, from the funeral all the way to this moment, I've been walking through a classic Sinclair set up, and Alex and I—even Grady this time around—fell for it.

If the deed said *descendants* on it all of this time, then Michael Sinclair's known about Emily—probably for years. And, like my entire four years of high school, he's been planning this and playing us like fools. He set up his dominoes perfectly for today, and he's somewhere nearby watching them all fall down, just so he can get his hands on my daughter.

I feel Alex's pistol, heavy and hard in my pocket, and I take it out and yank out the clip to count the bullets.

Eight. I think. *Eight shots.*

I shove the clip back in, repocket the pistol, and swallow down my tears hard as I make my voice as clear as a bell. "Tell me what happened, can you do that Emily? What happened at the hunting lodge?"

Emily's voice stays calm, which helps me stay calm.

"Grandfather woke me up when it was still dark. He

said he wanted to see my face. When Aunt Shelly tried to make it so he couldn't touch me, he hit Uncle Walt and Aunt Shelly and locked them in this basement place in the hunting lodge. And he even hit Nana...hard. She tried to protect me."

"I'm so sorry you had to see all of that. Did he hit you?" I bite into my tongue to ground myself and force the cries down my throat so Emily doesn't hear them.

"No. But he scared me. He said so many bad things I didn't understand about Daddy. He was pouring stinky stuff out of a big plastic can all over the room, getting everything wet. And then he lit a match and the stuff he was pouring caught the couch on fire. He told Nana to take me in the car while he finished up, but Nana didn't take me to a car. Instead she and I held hands really tight, and we ran away toward the lake instead. She said it was a good place to go if there was going to be a fire. And Mommy. The whole lodge was burning. I had to help Nana walk at the end because she was falling down. And then she fell into the boat but couldn't sit up. She said she was really dizzy. Before she fell asleep, Nana and I spread out a big tarp to hide under. I'm not supposed to move or peek out one bit. Is that right Mommy? I want to wake her up and ask again, but she's breathing funny. I'm afraid I'll hurt her. And she's bleeding on her head."

It's all I can do not to start bawling while pulling out my hair. Somehow, I keep it together. "Nana's right. Stay under the tarp, and do not look out. Please try to leave

Nana sleeping for now. I think it would be bad to try to wake her up anymore. Promise? For now…you just curl up and hug your knees and wait for me. If you hear my voice calling your name you come out. If you hear Grandfather's voice calling for you, or if you hear someone else say your name, even if they say they're the police, you stay hidden. Do you hear me?"

"P-p-promise." Emily says, sounding like she's about to break. "But—what if it's Daddy? Can I come out for him?" She whispers, all tears now.

"Only my voice, Emily, because you know it the best," I direct her. The sound of her small sobs nearly crumbling my soul.

"Don't cry, love. That might disturb Nana, and sleep is what she needs to get better. I'm walking to the lake now, and I'll be able to help her. Don't you worry, okay? It's all going to be fine," I lie, as I look up at the black, smoke-filled sky trying not to cough as the heated, debris-filled air closes up my lungs. I manage to keep my voice totally light while wondering what kinds of horrors my daughter saw at the hands of Michael Sinclair today. What horrors she won't be able to forget.

Unfortunately, I don't know what May's intentions are. It sounds like Michael Sinclair hit his wife hard enough to make her black out. Or it could be the smoke. But I've learned the hard way that physical violence is perfectly normal for him, and he doesn't hesitate to hurt his family.

Ha! Family. What kind of father fakes a death?

I've also learned that, bleeding or not, horrific injuries don't mean May Sinclair has stopped participating in her husband's evil plan. For now, the only thing I can assume for certain is she wanted to get away from the fire. There's a good chance she's been tasked to keep Emily alive and draw me into a trap. I don't have a way to confirm if May's faking that she's hurt or not. For all I know the woman is listening in and helping her husband track my location as well as Emily's right this very minute.

I think of the deed. I piece together what Emily's said to me, and while my daughter cries softly into the phone, I'm making my way down to the shore, uncaring that branches have scratched my face and my legs. I just want to get some sort of sightline on her. "Mommy, are you still there?"

I answer, shoving through the last of the bushes keeping me from seeing the lake. "Yes, baby. I'm close. Very close. Stay strong, okay?"

"Okay. Do you see me?" She asks.

"Almost," I lie, just in case Michael Sinclair or someone he's hired is listening in. I spot a lone canoe drifting into the middle of the glassy lake. Paranoid as hell now, I whip around, my eyes scanning for any movement behind me in case Mr. Sinclair has been watching me this whole time, luring me out into the open would be so like him.

In an instant, I realize the text messages sent to me that made my gut feel like something was wrong were never from Aunt Shelly at all. He was probably texting me all night long. Fuck, that evil man was probably setting up explosives inside the penthouse while Alex and I were there last night!

I stare at the bobbing boat, praying that May's not planning to hurt my daughter while shoving back images of Alex burning up in an explosion.

I swallow down the despair, and the self-hate for doubting my husband's intentions for even one second. A sick thought rolls through my mind over and over.

Will Emily watch me die today?

The smoke plume that's rising bigger and bigger now looks like World War III has erupted as the fire gobbles up this beautiful land. It's erasing the evidence of Michael Sinclair's murders.

It's erasing us all.

As if I've called the man to me on cue, I hear rustling in the brush above me, following the bush-wack trail of broken branches and upturned earth that I've just made as I tore through the woods to get to the shoreline.

Lowering my voice, I duck behind a rock and shove myself into an undercut indentation that's been carved out by an animal. I wedge my body under it, hiding myself the best I can. "I'm going to ask you to do something crazy now Emily. Something that will not sound right to you."

"What?"

"I need you hang up. You need to hang up now."

"I don't want to, Mommy. How will I talk to you?" Her fragile voice is raw with tears.

"You won't need to. I can see you. I'm almost there, but if we're talking someone might hear. Please Emily. The phone is dangerous for us. And you can't call me back, okay?"

"Okay," she says through a trembling sob."But wait."

"What?"

"I love you, Mommy."

The rustling in the brush above me grows closer. I pray it's only an animal running from the fire. I pray for a miracle.

"I love you too, Emily," I say clearly, despite the danger of it—because God help me, *my little girl.* What if this is the last time I'm allowed to say this to her. *What if...*

"I'll be right there," I add, more as a pep talk to myself, shoving my crippling panic away. "Stay hidden. Now. Hang up. Please...do it, Em, and whatever you do don't call me back."

She hangs up, and because I know she won't be able to resist calling me back in seconds, I power down my phone.

20.

ALEX, PRESENT DAY.

When Jojo isn't in the house, I force myself to believe she's marching toward our daughter. The alternative would be too grim. I pack a few supplies quickly and stash my messenger bag in the fireproof safe. Our documents might be the only things to save us, or to at least prove who was behind our murders.

I head through the back, grabbing our fishing rods as I go on an impulse to save them from the encroaching flames. I hit the path with long strides and pray with every step.

I see Jojo's hair first. A long, curling wisp of it blows up and plasters itself against the rock she's wedged herself under like it's a waving flag, giving her horrible choice of a hiding place away.

I stare at it for a moment, breathing in a surge of relief that I've found her so quickly. Then, on silent feet, I creep forward, working hard to stay under the canopy of the trees just in case the local news helicopter that's circling above, dodging in and out of the smoke plumes, is one that works for my father.

If he's alive, then of course it's not reporting any real news whatsoever. Whoever's in that thing is looking for footage that can be distorted or turned into lies. I wonder if Father's hired a sniper in that thing. At this point, anything is possible. My whole childhood I've been aware of how many millions have been paid to the police department for my father's sick reasons. I'm sure even more passed hands to pull off his death.

I glance around at the smoke that designates the fire line creeping toward the shore, and assess the amounts of ash falling around me and coating the surface of the lake, hoping the winds keep the fire burning in another direction—away from us, at least for now.

Helicopter and sniper worries aside, there is probably also a very real danger that my father or one of his fucking paid-off soulless minions is creeping nearby with the same orders to find, capture and kill Jojo.

I can't risk calling out to her, so instead I stash my backpack full of supplies as well as the damn fishing rods in the brush. I have no clue why I brought them with me—somewhere deep inside I must have felt like they would lead me to Jojo. I just couldn't just let them burn.

I creep as close as I can to the rock and silence my breathing as I crouch down to try to make eye contact with her. When I realize her entire body is contorted and all wrong under the rock—and when she doesn't move at all or appear to be breathing—my heart stops beating.

Is she dead?

Am I too late?

Is this not a hiding place?

Is it where someone's buried her?

Panicking, and needing to hold her body next to mine dead or alive, I reach and grab at her ankle with one hand, and then at an elbow with another, pulling her out with all of my might. As her body comes loose she erupts into movement, kicking and fighting with all she's got. I feel a deep bite hit the shirt over my forearm, tearing it just before her teeth sink in. At the same time, a gun gets shoved into my gut.

I whisper back fast, "Don't pull that trigger. It's me. Jojo—*please*. It's Alex."

At the sound of my voice she pulls the gun away and utters, "Alex," while her entire body grows limp. I keep my grip tight and drag her inside some thick brush next to the shelter of the large rock and then I let her go.

"I thought you were dead," we both whisper at the exact same time, our voices jagged and dry, meshed with the air we're pulling in. We're choking on the surge of heartbeats, hope and relief we've allowed our bodies to feel.

"I nearly shot you, I could've—killed you." Her body is trembling now as she loses control. She falls into me crumbling and sobbing quietly against my chest, and I find I can't hold her tightly enough. "And why didn't you just say my name first?" she accuses after a time.

Instead of telling her I couldn't breathe—that I thought she'd been murdered—I tell her only half of the truth. "I didn't want to shout out that I was there. It's not safe. We need to stay hidden."

She's gasping, trying to get control of her shaking. "I was so afraid—I thought..." A hard swallow chokes her and her eyes pool with heavy tears as she looks at me. "I was alone. I thought I'd have to do this alone."

"I had to make you think that," I add, trying to make her understand. "I couldn't let anyone know I was alive. I left my car and my phone, and I didn't call you on purpose because I wasn't sure what was going on or who was tracking me. I got a rental car one block away from where the explosion went off, then I went back to the house as quickly as I could to get you and Emily. I needed to get the gun and some supplies. Only, when I got home, you were gone, the gun wasn't there—and there's this fucking fire! Where's Emily?"

Her eyes connect to mine while one arm points toward the lake. "Emily called me. She's...she's there. I ran. I took the gun." She points again at the lake, her voice disappearing into her tears, all of her lost to what looks like full panic now. "She's *there*."

I lose my mind all over again. *Is she saying Emily's dead? Why is she pointing at the lake?*

I grip her tightly and give her a little shake. "You need to tell me more. Everything." We're both so gripped from adrenaline and relief that we're not making any sense. "Where's Emily? And Shelly?" I blink, helping her wipe away some of her tears. "Where's Walt? Because my father—Jojo—*my father...*"

I glance at her pale face, struggling for the right words to tell her the awful truth.

"I know," she bursts in. "Your father's alive."

Those horrible words, now said out loud, sober both of us into gaining back some control. "You dropped the deed on the way to the garage. First, I woke up and saw your note, and I thought you were fishing, maybe just saying goodbye to the lake. Then I read the small print on the deed, about how Emily's the heir to everything now, and I felt so stupid."

My heart hurts at her words, even the ones she can't quite say. She thought I'd tricked her. It hurts more watching her face replay it all.

"But then," she starts up again. "I saw the building— the penthouse—the top two floors are gone. I figured it out. Only, I thought it was May or Grady. But all along it's been your *father*. Alive." Her voice goes low with heavy despair. "We fell for it all over again, Alex. He tricked us—again. We're so stupid."

I shake my head, relieved as hell she doesn't think I've betrayed her—that she knows I'm with her, not with *him*.

"He fucked us all." I shake my head again. "Fucked even himself by faking his murder. All of this just to lure you here. And we're not stupid, Jojo. We just can't fathom his levels of darkness. Who knows how long he's known about Emily? This plan could have simmered for years," I whisper, gripping her hands in mine, willing her not to blame herself for any of this. "Grady—he killed himself. Saved me."

She gasps as I continue. "He actually saved my life. He wouldn't let me up in the building. He's supposed to be here instead of me, working for Father. Those were his orders. But he let me come instead. He didn't know Father was alive, either. Not until last night when our father appeared, giving him instructions. And new bruises and breaks."

Jojo's eyes are going black, as though she's going into shock. To keep her with me, I give her shoulders another shake. "You need to tell me all that you know right now—where the hell is *Emily?* Where?"

She points at the lake again, and my eyes fall to a lone, empty rowboat that has drifted about two hundred feet from us. "She's in that boat, hiding. She said she's with your mother. I think May's passed out. Emily says she's bleeding, and *sleeping*. She told me that your father hit May. I don't—I *can't* believe that she's truly asleep, though, because you know I can't trust her. Emily said your father locked Shelly and Walt in the cellar of the hunting lodge." She glances toward the massive smoke plumes in the sky. "They're both probably—"

Her swallow is hard.

"Don't say it." Quickly, I place my hand gently over her lips. "Shh. Shh." I soothe her. "We don't know that, so don't. Let's work on what we know—let's work on Emily, okay?"

She swallows, nodding and gulping back breaths and tears as she points at the boat again. "Alex...I told Emily I'm coming, and so I am." She pushes the gun into my palm and jerks my arm violently, trying to tug me out of the bushes. "I'll swim to her, and you cover me, and we'll get her."

I grip her tight and wrap her back into my embrace, but it takes nearly all of my strength to keep Jojo still. "It's a trap, Jojo. You swim out there, and someone will play target practice on you. Worse, they'll hit you and I'll come out to try to save you, and we'll both die—and Emily will be alone with my father."

Those last words finally register for her and she freezes.

"Can you hear the helicopter going around? That's not just for the fire. We need to stay hidden under these trees. We need to be smart about this. I have an idea. Stay here." I leap up and work my way back to my backpack and supplies, and her eyes light up when she sees the old fishing rods in my hands.

"Why do you have those?" she asks incredulously.

"I honestly don't know. I grabbed them on impulse as I was running out. I had this flash in my head—this idea that they'd burn in the fire. I couldn't leave them."

Jojo's already separated the rods and has handed me hers—the one that looks to be in better shape. I go to work untangling the bits of tackle that got snagged while I was running, and just as I'm looking around for a small rock to tie on as a weight for casting, she pulls the engraved lure from her front pocket and hands it to me.

Jojo's powered up her phone. "Hold on. I'm calling Emily; I'll put her on speaker."

"Mommy?" I hear the little voice coming through the speakers and nearly crumble. "You took so long," she accuses, voice raspy with her tears. "We need you. Nana 's awake now but she's sad. She says her head hurts, and we just need you."

"I'm so close, and I'm with Daddy," Jojo says, making her voice bright. "But don't tell Nana that Daddy's here. We want to surprise her. You stay down; he's throwing a fishing line with a hook at the boat right now, then we're going to reel you right in to us, okay?"

"Fishing for us? Okay." Her voice grows less worried.

I've got the lure attached, and I've cast. I miss on the first try and realize that I'm still going to need a rock tied on it to hook over the side of the boat so it will help me pull the boat closer. The tiny hooks on this lure won't do the trick. On my second try, I get the rock over the side of the boat, and the lure seems to have hooked onto the tarp as well. I'm momentarily distracted by the sound of my mother moaning in the background of Jojo's cell speaker.

"Can you ask Nana if she's able to talk to me?" Jojo asks Emily while I slowly reel in the boat, my heart flying with hope as everything holds tenuously and the boat heads in our direction.

"She's just crying, Mommy. I don't think she can talk."

"Okay, love. You're both so close. Tell her we're so close."

When the boat makes it nearly to the shore, Jojo whispers into the phone. "Emily, can you peek through the tarp and look for Mommy without moving the tarp too much—and if you see me, don't jump out until I say 'go,' okay?" she says, watching as the helicopter circles back in our direction.

I hear Emily's voice cry into the phone. "But what about Nana? She can't run or hop or jump. You'll need to carry her."

We both wait as the tarp moves and we see half of her little head appear. I nearly shout out as she gives us a wave.

The sight of her has set Jojo into action too, and she's bee-lining towards Emily. I don't call her back because the helicopter is not facing our direction anymore. I think it's going to be okay.

In seconds, Jojo's dropped her phone, waded in, has the tarp off of the boat and Emily in her arms. "Oh God, May!" She cries out, nearly sobbing at whatever she sees. "Alex is going to carry you out. We're going to get you to a hospital. May, thank you for saving Emily. Oh God, oh God..." Her voice goes up in a panic. "Stay with us, can you? We've got you. We've got you. It's going to be okay. Hang on. We're all right here. "

"Yes—we are. All here now? Aren't we?" My Father's voice—and the first blow from my father's crowbar—comes out of nowhere.

The second one I see coming—dead on, as does Jojo.

"Alex!" I hear her scream my name a breath before the stars and blur take over. *"Mr. Sinclair, no!"*

My father doesn't respond to Jojo; he keeps talking to me. "Except for that fucking idiot, *Grady!*" His voice ramps into a madman's shriek. "He's not here. He's betrayed me, hasn't he, Alex? Tell me what's happened? Did you at least kill him in a good fight, or did that motherfucker, sad excuse for a son of mine off himself by staying inside the explosion and send you out to kill me? What a joke that kid was from the moment he was born. Both of you. Horrible Sinclairs."

The third blow slams me in the chest so hard I hear ribs crack. I'm knocked flat. I assume he's been watching us this entire time, letting me get Emily to the shore. As usual, he's done this all so perfectly. The fire, the penthouse...even how he hit me with a crowbar like this, so not one ounce of air could be left in my body. Down to the detail.

My head is spinning, my ears are ringing, and I can't move my neck. Father's got the gun Jojo handed me earlier, and it's pointed at my wife and our daughter.

He's laughing as the flames from the fire barrel down behind us all. "What a nice day for a family reunion. Or...a family funeral? What do you guys think?"

He's acting how he always did—like a psychopath who's having a fun day at a lake torturing his *family*.

"Alex, do tell *your mother, your wife,* and your *dear little daughter* that I'm so disappointed in them." He scrunches up his face as he looks into the boat to eye my mother—his bloodied and battered wife. When she doesn't move, he rolls his eyes like he finds her annoying before stepping away from her and back to me.

"Oh May...I don't remember ever telling you to get into a boat. *Did I?* You and dear Emily," he sneers out. "You two should have been in my car. We should be long gone from this fucking fire, but instead, you've placed us all in danger."

My mother doesn't answer.

"Nana didn't want us to be burned in the fire," Emily calls out, defending her grandmother's actions. "It's safer by the water."

My father looks at Emily like she's an insect, like she needs a slap for speaking out of turn, and if I can't fix this, she will get one as soon as this is over. She'll get one every day of her life until she's trained. Emily, who doesn't know how to read my father's expressions, simply blinks up at him, expecting him to say something normal. But he doesn't. Instead, he kicks the side of the boat hard, and adds, "Too bad you're not already dead inside that boat woman, because now I'm going to have to come up with a plausible news story of what's happened to you—how you died on the day I came out of hiding." He chuckles. "But I'll figure that out, won't I? I always do. I have so many friends…"

"Emily." He orders my daughter in that voice that brings up every hair on the back of my neck and every single horrible childhood memory I've ever had. "Do you want your mommy and daddy to live today? If so, you will come right over to me now, and you will take my hand. Listen to your grandfather, Emily, and no one else dies…today."

Emily's eyes go wide, and Jojo begins to release Emily out of fear, and maybe…to save me. She's trying to save me, but this is not the way.

"No!" I croak, managing to pull in one rush of air before blood starts splattering out of my mouth. Apparently, more than just my ribs are broken, my father's fucked up my insides with that blow, too. "Emily, don't trust him! He's going to kill us. He's a liar. Jojo—Emily—run," I gasp.

Father walks over and kicks me hard, then levels the gun directly at my face. I say it again.

"Run!"

I hope and pray Jojo and Emily have taken my command to heart as I watch my father's fingers move on the trigger, and I close my eyes, imagining Jojo's beautiful face as I wait to die. As the sound of the too-close gunshot rings out, I jerk and go deaf—but then nothing happens. Nothing. Meaning…he's missed?

By the time I open my eyes, my mother's fallen on

her knees beside me, the small gun she's always kept in her purse since we were kids is clutched in her hands, and though I can hardly hear her words, I register the fire barreling down on us all.

"I'm sorry, Alex. I'm sorry, Alex. I had to, though. I've saved at least one of my sons. Forgive me for all of this horror…"

I roll to my side and make it to my knees, instantly realizing my father's been hit by a shot fired by my mother. She shot him directly between the eyes, leaving no room for error. She was taught very well, by the man lying in the dirt and brush. This is real. This is not pretend.

"We have to go…we have to go. Get back to the boat." I manage to gurgle out my words.

"Emily…can you get in the boat first?" I point at it, and because I can't stand at all, I do what I can and start crawling towards it, away from the raging fire.

Jojo gets her arms around my mother and somehow manages to get her back into the boat, then she returns to help me up and into the boat too.

We drift by the shore for a moment, all of us staring at the raging firestorm. The tree-tops are crowning down and shooting fire bombs of smoke and flame into the air. Emily's curled up in Jojo's lap, her eyes closed against the smoke. Jojo has her face pressed against Emily's. She's whispering beautiful words to her—affirmations that we are all safe and good now. She promises a rescue crew will come. She tells her that I'm okay, and that Nana's okay.

My mother starts shaking and seems like she's going to faint as the heat from the fire threatens to scorch us. Jojo picks up the paddles and starts rowing while I pull my mother into my arms to keep her upright and give her some comfort.

"Please...please hang on." Those words aren't just for my mom. They're for all of us.

A motorboat revs from the distance, then, like I'm deep inside a tunnel, I hear Jojo make Emily promise to never speak about what happened here at the lake. To never once mention that she met her grandfather, and to tell everyone we only got hurt because we all got trapped trying to escape this fire.

At first, Emily doesn't understand. She tells her mommy that people shouldn't lie. And she cries about it, which makes Jojo cry too, and shield Emily back into her hug.

I ask Emily to lie *for us*. That seems to help her understand, either that or she's so afraid that she's willing to accept anything we tell her now, as long as it doesn't come with sheer terror and cruelty.

Still, it makes me sad that we're asking Emily to lie for us. Lying—it's a very *Sinclair* thing to do...to make a *child* lie. I vow that it will be her only lie, and I pray harder than I've ever prayed that she can forget this day. Forget the crazy old man she met here in this place turned to ashes.

Mother clutches at me, shaking like she's going to pass out, and I cling to her in return, because I know I'm eventually going to pass out too. As the boat turns, we find we're both staring at my father's legs. We're both watching his body burn.

Somehow, she and I go to a new place together in that moment. Maybe we stare to be sure. Because we both have this feeling Father's going to stand up and start swimming after us.

But he doesn't.

EPILOGUE

JOJO, PRESENT DAY.

"Tell me again, Mommy. Tell me the story of how beautiful your mommy—*my* Grandma Ann was."

"As beautiful as you are," I say.

"Tell me how I have Grandma Ann's hair, and Nana's and Daddy's eyes. I like that part."

"Okay. Come here—snuggle in."

Emily's tiny hands wrap around my arms as she works her way up into my lap on our bed, Ajax snuggling in right behind her. She has trouble sleeping alone in her room at night, so Alex and I have gotten used to welcoming her into our room about an hour after tucking her in. I think Ajax likes it when she comes in here, too. That miracle dog is the one thing that survived that fire. He somehow knew to come home, and we found him curled underneath a support beam for the front porch, shaking and covered in mud and soot.

It was hard to feel at home in the lake house after the fire. So much of the forest is gone, and the landscape has changed forever. It's more than the marred hillsides and charred tree stumps, though. It's the ghosts that make it hard.

Alex offered to get rid of the house, or to give it to May and just let her live here. But I can't give this place up without a fight, even if it's a fight with our demons. As terrible as the end was here, the rest of the stories that make up this house—this lake and the land—are our very core.

I doubt I will ever be able to look over the water without thinking about my aunt and Walt. They lost their lives to the feud. But Alex built the most beautiful bench under my favorite tree, and he dedicated it to them. It looks toward the sunrise. He said that's because we are in a new day, and he knows I'll need the reminder of where we're headed—always forward, never back. One day I truly believe this place will be nothing but joy in our eyes, and I want to be able to hand it down the line to the Wallace-Sinclairs of the future. We changed the story of this place—we gave the feud an end.

"Well, the rumor was that when your Grandma Ann walked into high school on the very first day, no less than a dozen boys asked her to be their girlfriend."

Emily giggles because right now boys are gross to her. That will change for her one day, and I hope it's far in the future.

"How many is a dozen? Like...a hundred?" she asks.

Alex chuckles and throws his arms around both of us, rolling us back into the pillows and against his chest.

"Something like that," he hums, running his fingers through our daughter's silky hair.

Emily's mouth stretches wide into a yawn, and her fist comes up to twist in her sleepy, puffy eyes. I make eye contact with my husband and hold my finger to my lips, encouraging him to keep brushing her hair with his hand until he can lull her to sleep. It doesn't take long before her mouth is making the soft wheezing sound that we have learned is the sign that it's okay to whisper.

"She made it over an hour tonight," Alex says.

I smile on one side of my mouth.

"She'll get there. We all will." I let my head sink into the pillow as I scoot my leg and arm out from under Emily. Alex does the same so we're looking into each other's eyes while our little girl sleeps between us.

"I don't really mind having her here, honestly. I kinda like it." His crooked, goofy smile is all I ever dreamed of. He loves Emily so very much, just as I always knew he would.

"Yeah...but it makes it kinda hard to...ya know," I tease with a wink.

Alex sighs.

"Twenty-seven days and counting," he lets out in a whispered groan.

I laugh because that's a lie.

"You mean this morning doesn't count?" I challenge him.

"I'm just talking about nighttime sex. Morning sex is a totally different thing," he jokes.

I roll to my back and laugh a little harder, covering my mouth to not make a sound. I turn to the side again when I'm composed.

"You're a devilish thing, you know that?"

His eyes haze and one of his brows lifts to taunt me. I blink slowly in return and let my lips curl more, getting lost in his gaze while his eyes grow softer and he studies me. It gets silent for a while after that, nothing but our connected thoughts and stares appreciating what we are to one another. And we are so much.

We don't talk about it often, the moment I thought Alex was dead. It's hard for me speak about it because the feels are still so raw and real. My thoughts get tangled and the memories distort because for a small moment, despite how hard I tried to convince myself otherwise and hold onto hope, I was sure Alex was dead.

Even though I wasn't there when the penthouse exploded, I can see it happening when I close my eyes, and my nightmares area always one of two horrible things. Either Alex is leaping from the window up above just before the bomb goes off, dying a fiery death as he falls to the ground, or he's dying at the hands of his father, his face turning blue as his father's giant hands choke the life out of him.

Neither of those things really happened. That's what the therapist is helping me learn to believe. But the nightmares show up anyhow. When I wake screaming, though—Alex, he's always there.

I hold onto the feeling of his heartbeat, flattening my palm on his chest so I can feel him breathe and know he's full of life. Touching, it turns out, is one of the best forms of therapy for me, according to my therapist. Alex took that little bit of information quite literally, and he's not shy about touching me everywhere, but he's also always aware. He doesn't want me to ever feel like I'm being coerced or taken advantage of.

"You will always feel safe, and you are always in charge," he says every time.

He does make me feel safe. He always did, though. Even at our worst—at his worst—deep down I always knew he was my Alex, and whatever he did, he did it for me—for love.

"I love you, you know," I breathe out, lost in his tired eyes. They brighten at my voice and he hums.

"You may be the only one, but that's enough," he says back.

I give him a wry grin and glance down at Emily.

"All right, maybe two of you," he chuckles. His eyes settle in, lids heavy and heart full. He reaches over our daughter and runs his fingertips along my cheek, brushing back a strand of hair before moving his hand to my lips, grazing them with his knuckles. I kiss them as they pass and close my eyes wanting this to be the last thing I see. I want to paint my dreams with this vision right here.

"I love you too, Jojo. More than the sun."

THE END

ACKNOWLEDGMENTS

We hope you enjoyed this journey. These characters consumed us, as did the feud they survived. This story was all about the old-school romance vibes, and we hope you felt them. We'd be honored by your reviews and recommendations. And we're looking forward to making more magic together for you!

Thank you from the bottoms of our hearts to everyone who has ever lifted us up as authors, and who roots us on as a duo now. Our words would languish and our dreams would never get the chance to fly without you. This romance community is nothing short of awesome, and we are two lucky fish who get to swim in this amazing ocean. Tina Scott, Editing Addict, Autumn and Wordsmith Publicity, Kika MacFarlane, readers, bloggers, shouters, cheerleaders, friends—this list is endless and our love for you is just as bottomless.

Lastly, we said this in book 1, and it stands true for book 2. This is partly also dedicated to each other. To Annie from Ginger and to Ginger from Annie—loved every minute of this.

More than the sun...

ABOUT THE AUTHOR

Eliot Scott is the love child of bestselling authors Anne Eliot and Ginger Scott. You can find them at www.AnneEliot.com and www.authorgingerscott.com.

For updates on Eliot Scott projects, be sure to follow us at www.facebook.com/AuthorEliotScott.

www.ingramcontent.com/pod-product-compliance
Lightning Source LLC
Chambersburg PA
CBHW020230260626
47156CB00002B/620

* 9 7 8 1 9 3 7 8 1 5 1 7 2 *